# THE RESURRECTION OF SAM SLOAN

A Beyond Novella

# ERIN QUINN

THE RESURRECTION OF SAM SLOAN
by Erin Quinn
Copyright © 2015 Erin Grady

Material excerpted from *The Five Deaths of Roxanne Love*
Copyright © by Erin Grady

# Praise for the novels by Erin Quinn

"Quinn's Beyond series features a near-perfect blend of lush romance and steamy passion with a wonderfully creative paranormal world. [Reader's experience an] instantly engaging, heart-wrenching and ultimately life changing relationship...life, love, sensation and emotion through a heroine to whom everything is new and exciting." *RT Book Reviews*

"THE THREE FATES OF RYAN LOVE will throw you into a world of mythical proportions with Gods, demons, and seers like you've never dreamed possible. In one word — Amazing!" *Fresh Fiction*

4 1/2 star Top Pick: "Fascinating ...powerful ... beautifully wrought."
*RT Book Reviews on The Five Deaths of Roxanne Love*

Top Pick: "I absolutely loved The Five Deaths of Roxanne Love, and am eagerly anticipating the next book in the series." *Night Owl Romance*

"A richly developed time-swept paranormal series that should be on every romance lover's shelf."
*USA Today Books*

# CHAPTER ONE

THE REAPER TUCKED himself in shadow at the back of the room, waiting. It wouldn't be long. Already the rattle of death chased the breath from the body of the man in the bed. Already the grim shade of *mortis* crept over his skin. Sadly, he wouldn't regain consciousness before it was time to take him.

Unconsciousness stole the thrill from the reaping.

In the past few hours, nurses and the occasional doctor had bustled in and out of the room, checking vitals, offering sympathetic smiles to the soon-to-be widow sitting on the chair beside the bed.

A pretty thing, she stared at her dying husband with glazed eyes. Not weeping; not rejoicing. The Reaper had seen both in equal measures from other widows, but this one seemed to fall somewhere in the middle. Not yet ravaged by grief, and far from elated to be free of him.

She leaned back and stretched, groaning wearily as her strained joints creaked and her reluctant muscles gave way. Her shirt pulled tight over her breasts, the hem rising to flash a strip of pale flesh at her belly. Both drew his attention, until an exhausted sound pulled his gaze to her full lips, opened on a yawn. Her teeth were small and white, her tongue pink.

For time untold, the Reaper had moved in the world of humans, but rarely did he notice such mundane things as eyes or noses or lips and tongues . . . on this one he did. *Her* eyes were a peculiar shade of blue and green. Startling, like the woman herself.

The female stilled and her gaze moved slowly around the room, lingering for a moment too long on the corner where he stood.

Did she sense him?

"I don't know why I'm surprised to see you here," she said finally.

The Reaper stilled. Did she *see* him? She wouldn't be the first human to do so. He leaned forward eagerly.

"I think some part of me always knew."

Her gaze moved on and an odd disappointment filled him. Now, she stared at the silent man in the bed. The bandage on his head had been changed recently, but still it seeped over the wound the bullet had left.

"It was that dangerous edge that attracted me in the first place." She laughed. "I'm such an idiot."

Her head hung forward, and she sniffed before reaching for her dying husband's hand. "I want to be sad right now." She shook her head. "I mean, I am sad. But I'm not grieving. I'm not that much of a hypocrite. Hard to believe, right? After all these months of denial. I just thought . . . . You know me. Always looking for the fairy tale. I never quit hoping. But you broke my heart."

She fell silent and once again her gaze strayed, finding the Reaper in his corner. Pausing for a drawn moment before moving on.

"I hope there's a better place for you, Sam. One where you can figure your shit out. I'd tell you not to worry about the kids, but if you're in there, I'm pretty sure that's not your top concern. I know they're not my children, but I'll take care of them if Janet will let me. Now that you're . . . ." Her voice hitched. She cleared her throat. "She'll try to take them, and I don't know how I'll stop her."

The monitor beside his bed bleeped. The woman sniffed and looked up, dark brows pulled. Anxiously, her gaze shifted from the monitor to the man.

The time was near.

The machine made another strident sound and a nurse rushed in, checked something on the display, looked for a pulse, opened one of his eyes. Her expression said it all.

"I'll get the doctor, Maggie," she told the woman before hurrying from the room without an explanation.

*Maggie.* Her name was Maggie.

Maggie stared at the man again, the blues and greens darkening in her fascinating eyes as she came to her feet.

The Reaper stepped from his corner and moved to the bed. Maggie's gaze jerked to the corner and tracked back until it rested on him once again.

*Do you see me?* he breathed.

Her nostrils flared and a breath hitched somewhere in her chest just as two men in white coats hustled into the room. A different nurse followed, this one bigger than the first and all business. No sympathetic smile was given as she took Maggie's arm and moved her out of the way.

3

"Mrs. Sloan," the nurse said, "You might want to step out."

Maggie shook her head. "I'll stay."

The nurse gave a curt nod, and Maggie moved to the end of the bed where she could see without hindering their efforts. She didn't ask what was going on. Nor did she sob the usual, *will he be okay?* Samuel Franklin Sloan was going to die. She knew it as well as the Reaper did.

The doctors conversed in sharp tones, and the nurse bustled about efficiently. Maggie simply watched with that angry, mournful stare. The Reaper moved to stand beside her. Up close, her eyes shimmered with tears she was either too proud or too hurt to shed. She had long, dark hair that fell in a silky cloud to just below her shoulder blades. He touched it, wishing for the first time that he had the same senses as humans. Wishing he could *feel* the glossy strands.

She caught her breath and looked right at him. Her pulse beat a hard and erratic tempo at the base of her throat. Her eyes widened, the kaleidoscope of blues and greens mixing and changing. Her skin looked like pearl, her lips so soft he wanted to touch those, too.

The machines beeped frantically, drawing her back into the unfolding drama. The doctors began administering emergency measures, and two more nurses rushed in to assist. Maggie watched it all with an impassive expression, but he saw the panic she couldn't hide. He felt her bitter desperation, the guilt-ridden relief that it would soon be over.

It was time, but suddenly the Reaper wasn't ready to see the interlude end. One of the nurses pulled the blanket off the man and tugged down his gown so it bunched at his waist, unveiling his inert, muscular body. Even in death, he appeared strong, a big man with broad shoulders and a solid chest. Someone pushed a cart into the room, and Maggie shifted to the side to let them by.

She was almost touching him now.

Almost.

The temptation to bridge that gap became a seed, a sprout, then a vine that wrapped around him and choked out any thought to resist. In the moment of reaping, when he and the reaped would be one, he might touch her. He might *feel* her.

The Reaper shrouded himself in death and moved over Samuel Sloan, seeping beneath his skin to the soul that had brought this woman such complex pain. The man's brain still controlled his failing organs, still commanded his slowly beating heart and forced his weakened lungs to inflate, but his consciousness, that which made him the human, Sam Sloan, had long since ceased. The Reaper gathered up his soul and held tightly, emerging with just one goal.

Touch the woman.

He brushed his elusive shape against her like a dawn mist settling before a rising sun. He knew the moment—the very instant—she felt him. A fine tremble went through her body. Her lush lips parted, her breath caught.

She was warm, so very warm. So intricately alive. Flesh and blood, bone and hollow. The human's memory enhanced the sensations, until she became a bright, shining thing that blinded him with beauty.

The desire to see more, to feel more, became a burning need. Her soul was so lovely, so ethereal, so *alive* that it glittered, diamond bright—just there.

The Reaper reached. The Reaper touched. Deep inside him, he felt a stirring in the human he'd come for.

Somewhere in the room a doctor said, "Clear," and pressed paddles to the human's chest. Warning flashed red in the Reaper's mind a split second before searing pain sliced through the human, impaling them both.

The body on the bed jerked violently. The Reaper recoiled, and Maggie jumped back just as the doctor said, "Clear," once more. A second volt went through the human, through the Reaper, down to a place that shouldn't exist, galvanizing them both.

The Reaper knew the smell of fear in humans, but he'd never known it in himself until that moment when he felt the man's soul slipping backwards, felt the claws of it sunk deep inside him, thorns in the vine he himself had planted.

One last time, the doctor said, "Clear," and the die was cast, the fate was written.

The Reaper and Sam Sloan slammed back into the vessel from which they came.

# CHAPTER TWO

EVERY PART OF Maggie felt numb.

She sat in the waiting room outside of the Intensive Care Unit and stared at her clenched fingers. Over and over, those moments played. The doctors rushing in. The nurse telling her to step aside. That sense of someone watching over her, reaching out . . . *touching* her.

There'd been peace and promise in that moment, a sense of joy and homecoming. She'd felt Sam, the Sam she'd loved so desperately. But not only Sam, not *just* Sam. Something else had come with that touch, cool as a morning breeze, warm as a summer sun.

For that frozen second, she'd felt safe.

Until reality had crashed into her. The alarms beside his bed. The doctors and nurses trying to save him.

She'd cried out as the doctors had shocked his heart once, twice, three times. Someone had come in—the nice nurse, Leah, who always smiled and sometimes brought her coffee. She'd taken Maggie to the waiting room, asked if there was someone she could call. Promised to bring news.

Any moment now, they'd come to tell her Sam was dead. She still didn't understand her own feelings. Still couldn't piece together the last few days . . . the last few *moments.*

Had she felt Sam's soul leaving? Had an angel been in the room with them, ready to take Sam with it? Did she really believe in such a thing? Did it matter?

She shook her head, confusion and sorrow rolling over her in waves. What she'd felt had been dark and mysterious . . . seductive in ways she'd never be able to describe. And foreign—not just strange, but alien.

She covered her face with her hands. That shouldn't surprise her. Her relationship with her husband had been a whirlwind of strange excitement. They'd met, fallen in all-consuming lust, and married in the space of a month. She'd had a ring on her finger and a different last name before she knew anything about her new husband beyond the superficial. He was thirty-two, a single father and a successful engineer at a software company in Tempe, Arizona. His first disastrous marriage had ended with his ex-wife going crazy and trying to set their house on fire with his children inside it. She'd been committed to a facility for the mentally ill. Sam had taken the children and started over after the divorce.

He'd seemed a tragic hero to Maggie, triumphing over the wicked witch's curse, and she'd been so willing to believe that they were meant to be one another's happily ever after. Sam and his children *needed* her, and Maggie, who'd been on her own since her parents had died, needed to be needed.

But there the tale turned sour. Within weeks of moving into her small house and calling it home, Sam began to distance himself and the harder Maggie tried to reach him, the more distant he became. Strange bouts of paranoia had marked the path. At times, Maggie had suspected substance abuse, though she never knew for certain. The downfall came as quickly as the honeymoon.

Soon after, he left altogether. No explanation. No note or phone call. Not even an impersonal text message. Just gone, leaving Maggie and the kids to sift through the wreckage he'd left behind.

Until he'd been found in the parking lot of his apartment with a bullet in his brain and less than a ten percent chance of recovery.

Now, he was dead, or would be very soon, and she didn't know whether to grieve, rejoice, or spit on his cold body. How messed up was that?

"Maggie?" the nurse—Leah—said, coming to sit beside her on the nondescript sofa in the nondescript room. Her face was drawn, her eyes over-bright. She was shaking her head.

Maggie nodded, bracing for the inevitable. "Is he gone?"

Leah gave her a dazed smile. "No." A soft laugh accompanied the stunned expression. "He's awake. He's asking for you."

# Chapter Three

Even as Maggie pulled into the driveway six days later, she still couldn't believe she was bringing Sam back home. Alive. Just last week, she'd imagined herself parking the car with the small box of his ashes on the passenger seat. From the moment she'd received the call that her husband had been shot, that his wounds were likely fatal, she'd seen that end. Not this.

"We're here," she said, stopping the SUV, but not shutting off the engine.

Sam stared through the windshield with a hard expression that didn't quite hide the alarm she saw in his eyes. The doctors had prepared her for his memory loss, for the potential reactions he might have to it. Anger, frustration, and fear were common in victims of memory loss. Depression, equally so. But what she saw in his fleeting glance bordered on panic. For a moment, she wondered if he might bolt.

He took a deep breath and slowly let it out, turning his face away. Whatever he was feeling, he kept it to himself. Surprise, surprise.

Her many visits to the hospital had given her a small sampling of this stranger she'd brought home with her.

He knew she was his wife, yet he seemed very fuzzy on what that really meant. What it entailed, being a husband. Well, that hadn't really changed much, had it?

*Give him time . . . .* That's what the doctors had told her.

Sam had clear recall of his childhood and early adulthood. He had a vague memory of his first wife, but nothing concrete or clear. He knew he had children— Lexi and Justin—but not their ages or anything about them. He remembered meeting Maggie, but nothing after.

Of course, she distrusted the holes in his recall. How could she not? He'd left without reason. Now, he was back, without having to provide a reason for that either.

And sometimes he referred to himself in third person. Once, he'd started to say something that began with, "This human . . . ."

She couldn't even guess where that had come from or where he'd intended to go with it. He'd caught himself and changed course, becoming so agitated that the nurses had hurried in and finally sedated him.

A gunshot wound to the head and a week in the hospital had hollowed out his cheeks and added a dark shadow to his jaw, but it hadn't diminished the sharp gleam in his blue eyes or detracted from the masculine lines of his face. He was every bit as devastating as he'd ever been. She'd had plenty of reasons to fall so hard and fast for Sam Sloan.

"Are we going in?" Sam asked, shooting her a mystifying look.

Nearly a year had passed since their last curt words,

longer since she'd gazed into his beautiful eyes. Yet as she did so now, an uncanny feeling filled her.

It was as if a different man stared back.

Baffled, she shut off the engine and opened her door. She wasn't sure if he'd need her help so she moved to his side, but he'd already stepped out before she got there. He was such a tall, commanding man. The bullet was no longer lodged in his brain, but the injury made him understandably unsteady. Even so, the doctors had been stunned by his physical recovery. He was still strong. Able . . . and more than dangerous to her peace of mind. The weight he'd lost added to that perception. He looked edgy, mean, *hungry.* A street dog on the prowl.

His gaze found hers. So blue. So intense that it made her shiver.

"Do you need help getting to the front door?" she asked.

His lips quirked as he looked down at her five-two frame. The smiling glance was so reminiscent of the old Sam, the one she'd loved, that for a moment she could only soak it in. Obviously, he considered the idea of her helping his six foot, two hundred pound self amusing. She had a flashing image of him falling on her, leaving her like a splattered ink mark on the sidewalk.

"Okay, then," she said and walked ahead, refusing to give in to the compulsion to glance over her shoulder and make sure he followed.

The house was still and quiet when they entered. In an hour, she'd need to pick up Justin from the bus stop. He was in first grade. Eleven year old Lexi and her pack of mean girls wouldn't be caught dead walking with her step-monster. They'd take the long way home to avoid an accidental encounter. Like Maggie, both children were confused and conflicted about their father's homecoming, though Justin was too young to vocalize his feelings and Lexi too much a hormonal pre-teen girl to indulge in sharing at all.

"Do you want something to eat?" Maggie asked after an awkward moment of silence. "I made lasagna for dinner last night."

Which she knew he didn't like, but some passive-aggressive—*vindictive*—ogre inside had pushed her to make it anyway. If he couldn't remember being married, he shouldn't remember that either, right?

"Does he—do I like lasagna?" Sam asked.

"Not usually," she answered truthfully and then blushed like a school girl.

Sam cocked his head, watching her so intently that she had to fight the urge not to look away. He stood much too close and smelled way too good.

"Sit down and I'll make you a plate," she said. "If you don't like it, you can shove it across the table like you did the last time I made it."

She hadn't meant to say that. The doctors had told her that a calm, tranquil environment would enable him to find those memories he'd lost—unless, of course, it didn't. They hadn't expected him to survive the brain injury, let alone *remember*.

His gaze followed her as she moved to the refrigerator and pulled out the lasagna. She could feel it lingering on her stiff back, traveling down the curve of her spine. A tingle followed its trail.

"Did I really do that?" he asked after a moment, his voice soft. Husky, with just a hint of his Texas roots in it. Something else she'd fallen in love with, that deep, intimate timbre and the peek-a-boo accent that only surfaced when he was tired. Or aroused.

"Once," she answered with more attitude than she'd intended.

He frowned and his lashes lowered as he considered that, perhaps searching for the memory. After a moment, he looked up. "What did you do?"

Another flush heated her face. "I threw it at you." She shrugged at his startled expression. "Not one of my finer moments. I should have found a more adult way of handling it."

A slow grin spread across his face, the one that turned her insides to mush even now. "Did you hit me with it?"

She nodded. "Tomato sauce and cheese from head to toe. Now I make it just to spite you."

She hadn't meant to say that either, but this new, vulnerable Sam had her off balance and letting silence drape the spaces between them seemed like a bad idea. She cut a piece of the lasagna and put it on a plate, accidently splashing sauce on the counter and her shirt. Cursing, she put the plate in the microwave, licked a glob of sauce off her fingers and wiped up the rest, all the while hyper-aware of Sam tracking her every movement from his seat at the island counter.

The microwave dinged, and she set a plate in front of him with a bottle of sparkling water. He caught her arm before she could move away and towed her closer. With a gentle, warm hand he brushed something off her cheek. She glimpsed sauce on his finger before he licked it.

Watching her the entire time.

She was pretty sure all of her traitorous girl parts just went up in flames.

"Your lasagna is getting cold," she muttered, pulling away.

Finally, he lifted his fork and stared at the food for a quiet moment. Maggie steeled herself when he took a bite, chewing with that contemplative expression that made her want to ask what he was thinking. She suppressed the urge. Too many times, Sam's thoughts had come with sharp little barbs.

"His—my mother worked in the cafeteria," he said, his voice lilting up, as if this revelation were a discovery they shared.

"I didn't know that. You never had much to say about your family." Even when she'd asked, which she'd done a lot.

She'd always thought family was the nucleus of who and what a person was. Even before her parents had died leaving her all alone in the world, she'd found the subject endlessly fascinating.

Sam nodded and took another bite, lashes lowering as he chewed and swallowed. "I was ashamed of her," he said finally, his words a peculiar mixture of wonder and fact. "She worked at my school."

Maggie poured herself a glass of water and leaned against the counter, undeniably curious.

"She used to bring the lasagna home," he said, taking another bite. "It was her favorite."

"And you grew to hate it?" she asked.

He shook his head. "Just her. It was always my favorite, too."

She stared at him, glass half-raised to her lips. "I can make you a sandwich if you'd prefer."

He took another bite. "She's dead, now."

"I knew that. She died when you were a boy."

"Last year."

"I'm sorry?"

"She died last year. May."

"But . . . ."

They'd gotten married in April. Yet he'd never said a word. His mother had *died* and he'd never bothered to mention it. She hadn't thought he could hurt her any more, but she'd been wrong.

"Is that why you left?" she demanded.

He blinked at her and his brows pulled together in consternation. His eyes shifted as he scanned his memory for answers.

"I don't remember leaving."

She sighed and rubbed her face with her hands. She needed to get some distance—from him, from her feelings about him.

She cleared her throat and looked away. "You always made it sound like she died a long time ago."

"I don't know why," he said simply.

16

Maggie nodded. Silently, she watched him eat, his aversion to the dish apparently banished now. He ate slowly, savoring each bite. When he paused to take a drink, he looked up and caught her staring. And blushed. Sam Sloan blushed. In the world of crazy that life had become, this was an anomaly she couldn't reconcile.

"Tell me about us," he said.

Maggie stiffened. "What do you want to know?"

"Why did you marry me? Am I rich?"

"You think I married you for money?"

"Did you?"

"No." She took a deep breath. "The doctors told me not to upset you."

"And telling me the truth about us will do that?"

"I don't know, Sam. I haven't seen you in months. I don't even know who you are."

He waited, quizzical. Pretty much the opposite of upset. He gazed at her with the dispassion of a detective, waiting for a witness to respond.

"I have to pick up Justin in a few minutes," she said, turning her back.

"You're fond of h—my children."

Half statement, half question. She drew in another steadying breath and nodded.

"Justin's not even six. He doesn't remember much about . . . before."

And he loved her unconditionally.

"Lexi is—" *hormonal*—"almost twelve. She remembers everything."

Lexi was hard to love and yet, at times, there were

glimmers of the lost child inside. Maggie understood that inner child. She had one like it inside herself. The children needed her almost as much as she needed them.

She faced Sam again and her gaze was caught by his impossibly blue eyes. What was he thinking?

"Yes," she said thickly. "I'm very fond of them."

"You said you'd keep them, take care of them."

At her blank look, he went on.

"You said it in the hospital."

He'd heard that? What else had he heard?

He took his last bite, wiped his mouth with his napkin and smiled. "That was delicious, Maggie," he said.

"Thank you." Inside, she felt raw. Exposed. She swallowed the lump in her throat and turned away. "I need to go meet Justin's bus now. Why don't you rest? The doctors said you should take it easy."

He eyed her, making her feel like he could see right through to all the churning emotions inside. Before he could say anything else, she strode to the door, not stopping until she was outside on the front porch. She leaned against the railing, trying to catch her breath, trying to understand who the man in her kitchen was and why she saw a stranger when she looked in his eyes.

# CHAPTER FOUR

MAGGIE TOOK ALL the warmth from the room when she left. At least that's how it felt. It had been the same during the interminable time he'd spent in the hospital, waiting for her to visit. Dreading the moment she'd leave.

The Reaper stood, rinsing his plate in the sink as he'd seen humans do before. He knew that Sam Sloan wouldn't have bothered and wondered why he should either, but it seemed a little thing to do, and it would keep her off balance until he could find a way out of this situation.

He stepped through the rooms, feeling the disjointed memories of the man whose body he occupied echo with his footsteps. Alone, the panic seeped in.

He still didn't know how it had happened. He remembered stepping in—early because he'd *needed* to touch Maggie for reasons he still didn't fully understand. Half in, half out, he'd bridged the gap between them. Even now, he could feel that sense of *her*. The wonder, the beauty, the draw that had kept him holding on when he should have let go and taken both himself and the dying Sam Sloan to the Beyond.

The pain had come fast and hot, electrifying. He'd felt the human's body seize, felt the clutch of Sam's consciousness as it sparked and then . . . the inferno had seared him, melted him, melded him into something he wasn't.

Now here he was, trapped in this alien body.

And still thinking about touching the woman.

As far as he could tell, no one in the Beyond knew he was here. Reapers were a common, expendable thing, not unique enough to even bear a name. Not like angels or demons that were tallied and tracked, albeit with limited success. No rescue party would be coming to help him get back to the Beyond, where he belonged. He'd have to find the way on his own.

The logical solution would be to kill the vessel that lodged him and free them both. But in those seconds when he'd tried to pull Sam's soul from his body, a sense of wrongness had enveloped him. A tainted hue had smothered Sam's light—a corruption of some sort that had taken flight in the final moments, leaving Sam's soul damaged and weak.

There were several possible explanations for what the Reaper had seen and felt. Possession was the most likely. Sam could have sold his soul to one of the many demons of the Beyond, and that dark veil that had doused his light could have been the courier come to claim it. Perhaps the events that followed, the electrifying pain, the entrapment in this body . . . that had trumped the demon's plan. A soul could only be taken in death and Sam was still alive.

It all made sense, except it hadn't *felt* like a demon

and that intrigued him. What else had the power to control a human soul? Equally important, had Sam been aware of it—whatever the illusive *it* was? Had he consented and let it in?

*Is that why you left?*

Those five words spoken by Maggie had been so pain-filled, so angry. So telling. He'd wondered at the estrangement between Sam and his wife. He'd puzzled over the stupidity of the human male.

To be near Maggie was to yearn to touch her. Each touch made him long for another. He wanted to press his mouth against hers more than he wanted to breathe. He wanted other things, too. Things he could barely conceive.

This, Sam had left.

He shook his head, fighting the urge to dwell on that. Sam's foolish decisions were not his concern. Escaping this human casing was. Yet . . . .

Killing the vessel would solve the problem and send him back where he belonged. It would release Sam's damaged soul and leave it to whatever fate awaited in the Beyond. But it wouldn't answer the question—what taint had darkened Sam Sloan's soul in the first place?

Nor would it appease the hunger inside the Reaper, the hollow need for the woman that was too great to ignore. Despite the fact that being contained by this body felt unnatural and a part of him yearned to shed it, the very idea of leaving before he had the chance to understand, to satisfy his desire, filled him with frustration. He wouldn't—*couldn't*—do it.

He stopped his relentless pacing, decision made. He would delay the destruction of this body until he knew more about the corruption he'd sensed . . . and until he could quench his thirst for Maggie. He would have the woman first. Return to the Beyond after. In that order.

"Maggie," he said aloud, as he'd done in the hospital when he'd waited for her.

He moved to the window. She was coming back, strolling down the sidewalk holding a boy by the hand. As they walked, the child spoke with animated gestures, and she listened with undivided attention, a slight smile on her lips.

Until she looked up. Until she saw him.

She froze. So did the Reaper, while all the breath left his borrowed body.

What was she thinking? How could just a look make every inch of him feel hard and hungry?

Mouth dry, he waited for her to come to him.

# CHAPTER FIVE

THE AFTERNOON AND evening had crept by, marked by Sam's veiled glances and Maggie's overwhelming awareness of his every move. He always seemed to be too close, too observant, too big . . . too masculine. When he was near, she felt it beneath the skin. It had always been like that between them, even in the end.

They had breakfast for dinner, usually a favorite, but as Maggie moved around the kitchen, Sam seemed to be everywhere she turned. In her way. Making her agitated and so aware of him that her nerves buzzed. Every time he touched her—which was pretty much every chance he got—he scattered her thoughts and turned her into a bumbling fool. Once he reached around her at the sink, and she nearly melted to the floor in a boneless puddle. If anything, this new version of Sam—Sam 2.0—made her attraction to him more lethal.

The kids buffered some of the tension, but they also contributed to it. Lexi texted continuously as she pretended to do her homework instead of watching the stranger in their midst with the same suspicion as Maggie did. The last time Sam had been home during an evening like this had been nearly a year ago. The memory was peppered with his short temper and impatient pacing from window to door. He'd been waiting for a call and as soon as it came, he'd left as abruptly as he'd arrived.

And only returned to pack a bag.

Maggie didn't chastise Lexi for her disrespect now. Sam might seem like a changed man, but no one could erase their past, no matter how much they wanted to. Lexi had a right to her anger. So did Justin, but he was too young to know it.

"Does your head hurt?" Justin asked, looking up from the picture he'd been drawing to eye the bandage covering the shaved spot just over Sam's left ear.

Sam touched it. "Some."

"Who shot you?"

It was the question of the hour. The police had been to the hospital several times, asking the same thing, interrogating, trying to trip him up and expose the amnesia thing for the lie they suspected. Sam had been shot point blank. How could he *not* remember who'd done it?

One of the detectives had stood in front of Sam, demonstrating just where and how close the shooter would have been when he pulled the trigger, but nothing seemed to jar his memory, and each time they asked the question, Sam grew more confused. Agitated.

"I don't remember who shot me," he told his son.

She almost believed him.

"How come?" Justin asked.

Sam shrugged. "I just remember waking up in the hospital and seeing your mom."

"*She* was there?" Justin asked with a scowl.

For a moment, Sam looked uncertain.

"I'm not their biological mother," Maggie reminded him gently.

Memory nudged, he nodded. "I meant you," he murmured, gaze intent on her face.

Justin let out a breath. "That's good. *She* would have made you cry."

Justin's mother made everyone cry eventually. Maggie had only met her once, but Janet had a sly way of ferreting out the facets of fear that lurked in a person's sense of self. Maggie's stomach still clenched when she thought of the time Sam's ex-wife had come to her house shortly after the wedding, before things had gone bad.

"I thought it was a rumor," Janet said when Maggie opened the front door.

Maggie had assumed Janet was still living at the facility where she'd been committed. Still, she'd known instantly who the beautiful woman on the front step was. Lexi had her eyes and mouth. Justin, the thick blond hair.

"The children are at school, Janet," she'd said calmly, pretending that she felt no threat in the other woman's appearance even though her heart had been racing.

"I came for you, Miss Fancy Pants," Janet had replied with a dimpled smile. "Enjoy my family while you can. They won't be yours for long."

Maggie had wanted to scoff or return a snide comment in kind. But Janet had effortlessly pricked a festered wound. In the deepest, darkest corner of her mind, Maggie had been waiting for something like this, convinced that so much happiness was simply an invitation to heartbreak. Maggie had plenty of experience with losing things she loved. The moment had felt portentous. Later she would realize it had been a harbinger of the future.

Now, Justin returned his attention to his school project—what he planned to do over summer vacation. So far he'd drawn a picture of himself, his sister, and Maggie on a sandy beach.

Reluctantly, Maggie glanced at the clock. It was almost nine-thirty, long past Justin's bedtime. Selfishly, she'd let him stay up late to postpone the dreaded moments when she'd have to be alone with Sam.

"Time to clean up, buddy," Maggie said.

Justin grumbled, but it had been an exciting day and he was tired. Sam watched with interest as Maggie helped Justin write his name on the bottom of his picture before they gathered up all of the crayons and put them back in the box. Lexi slammed her books shut and crammed them into her backpack. She went up to her room with a mumbled, "'Night."

"Good night, Lexi," Sam answered, startling them all.

He followed Maggie and Justin upstairs when they went—too close once again—and leaned against the door jamb while she helped Justin brush his teeth and get into bed. They'd been reading Justin's favorite—for the third time—a mystery about three kids, two dogs and a babysitter in a haunted house at night.

Justin said, "I don't want that one," though, when she picked it up off his nightstand.

Surprised, Maggie answered, "Finally tired of it?"

"No. Just don't want to be scared."

The story had more humor than thrills, and he knew it by heart. Wondering what caused his change of mind, she picked a Dr. Seuss book from the shelf and sat on his bed.

"Do you wanna come in and hear the story?" Justin asked, looking past Maggie to where Sam stood at the door.

Maggie glanced over her shoulder, sure that the invitation would do the trick and convince Sam to find something better to do. Instead, he came in, filling the small room, looking big and male and completely out of place among the toys and stuffed animals scattered about. The shadow of his beard gave him a hard, disreputable appearance that trilled against every nerve ending. He'd showered earlier, and now she caught a whiff of his expensive cologne. She'd always loved the way Sam smelled—even when she'd been actively hating his guts.

She'd packed up most of his things and stored them in boxes in the garage, but his cologne stayed in the mirrored cabinet. In weak moments, she let herself remember how it had felt to press her face against his skin and breathe that scent in.

She held her breath when he sat beside her on the bed. Too close, of course. She could feel the heat of his thigh against hers.

The book was short but it seemed to go on forever as her awareness of the large man beside her reached excruciating levels. Each time his glance strayed to her face, she felt a flush follow, scalding hot. Every shift in weight brought her closer to him, made her want to jump to her feet and bolt. With relief, she declared, "'And will you succeed? Yes! You will, indeed! (98 and 3 / 4 percent guaranteed.),'" and looked up just as Justin's eyes drooped shut with only a few more sentences to go. Smiling, she closed the book. Pressing a gentle kiss to his forehead, she turned on the nightlight, switched off the lamp and left the room.

Sam came right behind her.

Nervously, she made her way to the master bedroom. Sam and the children had moved into her small house after they'd wed. The plan had been to fix it up and sell it so they could buy a bigger place—one with enough room to grow their family.

At least he'd fixed the drippy bathroom sink before he'd lost interest in that goal. She didn't know where he'd been sleeping for the last year, presumably the apartment where he'd been shot. She'd given up caring. At least, that's what she told herself.

The house only had three bedrooms, a fact she'd been worried about since the doctors had said to bring him home. Sam followed her into the master bedroom now, as if he meant to sleep there. With her.

Something deep inside turned traitorous at the thought.

Determined not to show just how disconcerted she was, Maggie moved to the bed, took her sleep shirt from the nightstand drawer and grabbed her pillow. She'd curl up with Justin tonight, though for such a little boy, he was a terrible bed hog. She'd be exhausted in the morning.

"Just let me grab my toothbrush," she mumbled as she brushed past Sam on the way to the bathroom.

He caught her arm, stopping her. Surprised, she looked up into those compelling eyes. "We don't sleep together?" he asked, a shade of disappointment in his tone.

"We don't live together," she answered pointedly.

He had that lost, panicky look again. It staunched the harsh words that wanted to follow. She swallowed, realizing just how bitter she'd become.

"I thought you'd be more comfortable if you had the bed to yourself," she said instead.

His gaze made a lazy search of her face, long lashes casting shadows in the hollows beneath his eyes. He looked vulnerable and dangerous all at the same time.

"I wouldn't be," he said softly, tugging gently on her arm, pulling her so she stood rebelliously in front of him.

Only not all of her was rebelling. A conspirator within just sighed, *finally*.

She narrowed her eyes, trying to peer through the many layers of façades to the truth. "What are you doing, Sam? I mean, other than trying to freak me out with all these soul-searching looks and touching?"

He tilted his head, that thoughtful expression back on his face. "You don't like me to touch you?"

Just the opposite. Even now, she craved it.

"It's not that. It's just that—Sam, I know you don't remember and holding you responsible for the things you did when you have no recollection of them—it feels wrong. But . . . I *do* know. I remember all of it. I can't pretend I don't."

He caught his lip with his teeth, nodding in that inquisitive way. "I'm not a good guy," he said at last. "Am I? In the hospital, I heard you say that."

She looked down, flushing as she remembered her harsh words. "I shouldn't have said that. I was just mad at you for dying."

He shook his head and cupped her face with his free hand. He still had her arm grasped in the other, but she could pull away if she tried. Fool that she was, she didn't.

"No, you weren't," he said in that low voice. "You were mad at me for taking so long to do it."

"That's not true," she lied.

"I think it is. You don't even like me."

She swallowed. *Like* was too ambivalent to describe anything she'd *ever* felt for him.

"You haven't given me a whole lot of reasons to like you, Sam."

"Why haven't you divorced me then?"

Her throat felt like it was coated in tar that sucked down the words she tried to speak. "Justin," she managed at last. "Lexi. Mostly Justin, since Lexi can't stand me. She needs me though."

His blank look angered her.

"They aren't mine, Sam. Before you left, you made it perfectly clear that I'd never see them again if I went anywhere. Not that I needed the threat. I couldn't abandon them to you and—" *Your vicious ex-wife—* "Janet."

He nodded, his expression more pensive than

shamed. She shouldn't be surprised. Sam and Janet had been a matched set.

"Do you remember what she's like?" Maggie asked.

"Only her name. Not her face. Nothing else."

Truth? Lies? Did it really matter?

"I'll sleep with Justin tonight," she said, pushing past him. She was dangerously close to tears and furious with the emotional tornado spinning inside her. It wasn't fair . . . this moment. Any of the moments since he'd awakened from certain death. Asking for *her*. Watching her with those beautiful eyes, tracking her movements— as if where she was, what she did—mattered to him.

She scooped her toiletries off the bathroom counter and into a travel bag she kept under the sink, and then returned to the bedroom for her pajamas and pillow. Sam hadn't moved.

"Maggie?" he said softly.

*Don't turn around. Don't look at him. It will only hurt.*

She let out a deep breath and faced him. "What?"

He shook his head, hands coming up from his sides. "Staying for the kids . . . that's not the right reason to hang on. I'm sorry he—*I*—made you make that choice."

He looked as stunned by the declaration as she felt. Her jaw dropped and the tears she'd valiantly tried to hold back, pooled in her eyes, blurring her vision. "Who *are* you?" she demanded in a broken voice.

He blinked, his expression once again mystifyingly panicked. As if he'd stumbled into a house of mirrors and no longer knew which reflection to believe and which to fear. His mouth moved over silent words before at last he spoke in a low, somehow damning voice. It was filled with that familiar, possessive tone, that hint of Texas she'd fallen in love with. The one she'd let talk her into anything.

"I'm your husband, Maggie."

He took a step forward, invading her space with his size and scent and blue, blue eyes. Anger lurked in their depths, mixing in the tide pool of longing that made no sense. He'd abandoned *her*.

He wasn't touching her yet, but he stood so near, she felt his breath at her temple. She curled her fingers into her palms, willing herself to stand strong and straight. He wasn't the man to lean on in a moment of weakness. She knew that. And yet, she'd missed him so much.

He bent his head until his lips almost grazed her cheek. If she turned her face, his mouth would be on hers. He took a deep breath and his eyes closed, as if the smell of her intoxicated him.

"Funny how a scent can make a man remember," he murmured. "I can see you that first day, coming out of Starbucks, yours arms filled with books . . . ."

She could see it, too. Juggling real estate exam test prep books and the last few swallows of a triple shot Americano, she'd run straight into him—the kind of thing that happened in movies or sitcoms. But it had been real. Her. Him. So very real.

He'd been dressed in blue jeans and a white button-down shirt with a crisp collar and untucked tails. His dark hair had been swept back by the wind, his cheeks freshly shaved. He caught her in his arms before she hit the ground, her books flying everywhere, coffee splashing their shoes. And he'd held her for just a moment too long.

That was the first time he'd stolen her breath.

"You were studying for a test," he said, trailing off as he tried to remember.

"My real estate license."

"Did you get it?"

"Yes."

"Is that what you do now? Sell houses?"

She nodded at the same time he leaned in. His nose brushed hers, his lips a whisper away. She had to fight the urge to bridge that gap. She wanted to feel those words he didn't say, she wanted to taste them. Caught in the throes of indecision, his breath became hers, a gossamer intimacy gathered tight around them.

Some remnant of self-preservation pushed her back. The first step was painful, but with distance came clarity. For Sam, too, it seemed. He rubbed his face, let out a deep breath and headed for the door.

"You can have the bed, Maggie," he said, his voice rough around the edges. "I feel like I'm finally waking up. I don't want to go back to sleep."

Maggie's mouth was open again. His gaze lingered on her face before he gave her a lopsided grin that slammed her heart against her ribs, and left the room.

# CHAPTER SIX

THE REAPER PROWLED downstairs, playing the moments with Maggie in his head and analyzing every reaction—hers and his. The heart in his chest had been beating so hard it caused him pain and his breath had been short and lacking in oxygen. He didn't understand these human reactions, yet he knew without a doubt that *she'd* done that to him. He suspected he'd returned the favor, but he couldn't be certain. She was a mystery. One he shouldn't want to solve.

But he did. Badly.

His human skin no longer felt alien. The body seemed to have relaxed, stretching to accommodate its new occupant. More and more frequently, he could feel the human inside him. No clear memories, but a sense of right and wrong remained . . . impressions of how the Reaper *should* react . . . and a deep-seated confirmation of all the feelings he still didn't understand.

The Reaper was at once grateful and resentful of the "assistance" these memories provided. Everything here was new, awkward and foreign. He wasn't just a stranger in a strange land. He was a stranger in his own skin.

*Who are you?* Maggie had asked.

The question hovered at the edge of his consciousness, unanswered.

Yet despite all that, very little of Sam Sloan remained inside. Just a damaged soul and the bits and pieces that sparked whenever Maggie was near. Like burrs, they lodged in their shared psyche.

Twice, the Reaper felt them burrowing deeper, tearing the thin membrane that kept him separate from the human. Bleeding over . . . bleeding out.

In the beginning, he'd felt odd answering to the human's name. Now when she called him Sam, it no longer felt strange to answer.

He crossed to the kitchen and opened the refrigerator. Milk, he didn't care for, but Maggie had poured him a glass of orange juice that had tasted so good he craved more. He found the carton and drank straight from it, before bending down, searching for the leftover lasagna or maybe a few pieces of bacon from their "breakfast for dinner" which had been amazing.

A sound behind him spun him around. He stood in a pool of light from the open refrigerator. Beyond it, deep shadows cloaked the corners of the kitchen and glanced off the steel appliances. White shutters had been snapped shut against the prying eyes of night, but pinpoints of light shone at the gaps between the slats. He shut the refrigerator door, dousing the bright glow, and moved to the sliding glass door behind the round kitchen table. The vertical hanging blinds covering it clattered when he pushed them aside for an unobstructed view.

A cinderblock wall framed a grassy backyard with

two shade trees. A compact patio with a wrought iron table and chairs overlooked a pond-sized swimming pool with a glassy surface and dark waters. To the right, an elaborate swing set with a bright yellow slide hunkered beneath a striped canopy. Sam's memories told him the covering was necessary. Arizona sunshine could be lethal to human skin. Something glittered from inside the fort at the top of the slide. He looked closer. Cat eyes.

Minnie—a perplexing name for a cat the size of a panther—gracefully bounded down the slide and sashayed to the corner of the patio where the creature gave him a disdainful look and began cleaning her paws.

The Reaper smiled. The cat was quite brave with a wall of glass between them, but when he'd walked through the front door, she'd bolted like her tail was on fire. One glimpse of fluffy black and white fur and the *flap-flap* of the swinging pet door was all he saw. As if hearing his thoughts, she hissed and charged at him, coming to an abrupt stop a few feet away, back arched, tail bent and fur on-end as she bobbed on her paws.

Surprised she'd come even that close, he reached for the lock, intending to step outside and challenge the insane feline. As he shifted, a reflection in the glass popped into startling focus. A pale face, right behind him.

He spun to see it, but no one was there and only the quiet stood in his wake. Frowning, he moved to the arched opening that gave way to the family room. His footsteps whispered over tile and carpet as he searched for the source of his disquiet. The part of him that remained ever *Reaper* began to ping in a steady signal.

Something dead this way came.

He smiled grimly. Foolish spirit.

Nothing but more velvety silence waited in the family room, yet the gloom seemed to shudder and take on a tight, expectant feel as he advanced on it. The chairs and couch—piled with the pillow and blankets Maggie had given him—loomed in the dark. The Reaper turned in place, trying to distinguish shadow from shade. It was here. He felt it even if he couldn't see it.

Slowly, he scanned from corner to corner while all of the hairs at the back of his neck rose in a human reaction that unnerved him. A movement caught his eye—pale and quick as lightning, it was there and gone before he could be certain he'd really seen it. A cold gust brushed against his face, a feather touch trailed down his spine.

"Be careful," a small voice said, startling the Reaper and making him jump like a frightened human. Disgusted with himself, he looked up and spotted the boy sitting at the top of the stairs.

The child looked tiny in the endless dark, his face a pale orb marked with huge eyes and a pink mouth.

"Why aren't you in bed?" the Reaper asked.

"*She* was in my room."

He'd said *she* in that same tone when the Reaper had mentioned the boy's mother, but what he sensed in the house now wasn't human. Not anymore.

"Who?" he asked.

The boy shook his head. "She'll hurt me if I tell."

The Reaper moved to the foot of the stairs. "Come

down."

Cautiously, Justin stood and came down the stairs. All knobby bones and sinew, he wore an oversized t-shirt with a picture on the front of a yellow, one-eyed, monocled creature shaped like a capsule, holding a banana. The Reaper didn't understand the reference. Justin clutched a fluffy toy dog in one hand and a blue blanket in the other. The blanket trailed him all the way down.

The boy stopped just in front of him and tilted his head way back so he could look into the Reaper's face. The two stared at each other for a long moment.

Finally, the Reaper asked, "This thing you saw . . . do you see it now?"

Justin looked around the room, craning his neck to see past the Reaper's legs, but never moving around him.

"Not now."

"But it was in your room?"

Justin nodded fearfully. "Last night, too."

"Not before that?"

The boy shook his head vigorously.

The Reaper glanced up the stairs then back to Justin. "Go sit on the couch. I'll look."

"You're not afraid?"

"No."

"But you believe me?"

Justin's voice was tremulous, his eyes like saucers, his expression so earnest it touched something inside of the Reaper.

"I believe you."

Justin didn't move from where he stood and the Reaper wasn't sure what to do next. "Go sit down," he said again.

"I'm afraid."

Sighing, the Reaper squatted beside the child. Instantly, Justin stepped forward into the vee made by the Reaper's spread knees. As if some magic incantation had been spoken, the Reaper's arms went around his thin frame at the same time Justin wrapped his about the Reaper's neck. The child felt so fragile in his hold. So easily broken.

"Do you want to come with me?" the Reaper murmured.

Justin nodded. "Only if you promise not to leave me there."

The Reaper stood and the boy's legs wrapped around him like some pale monkey. He tugged the blanket up so it was against his cheek as he laid it on the Reaper's chest. Somewhere deep, a part of the Reaper he didn't recognize, awoke. Was it the human he felt? He searched the few memories that lay dormant within Sam's mind, but he couldn't find any that related to the child in his arms.

Effortlessly, he carried Justin up the stairs and down the hall. No light showed from under the door to Maggie's room but a gray glow came from beneath Lexi's door.

"She's binge watching Sons of Anarchy on her computer," Justin whispered. "She's not supposed to."

The Reaper nodded. He had no idea what that meant,

but clearly there were more important matters to deal with. Like a ghost in Justin's room.

Maggie had left a nightlight on, and the small bulb cast a dim glow out to the hall. Justin buried his face in the Reaper's shoulder as they entered the room. A plethora of toys covered the floor by the window, spilling out of a bin that was obviously meant to contain them, and spreading like a stain to the closet.

"Where did you see her?" the Reaper asked softly.

Justin pointed at his closet. Quietly, the Reaper approached, checking the corner by the brightly patterned curtains before he opened the closet door. Justin made a soft gasping sound and hid his face again.

The Reaper stepped in, keeping Justin secured with his right hand and using his left to push the clothes aside. It was cold in here, cold enough to see his breath. Justin began to shiver and whimper. The Reaper rubbed his back and made *shhhh* noises at him.

The thing was here. The cold, dank odor left little doubt. It was newly dead by the smell. And angry. He could feel that, too.

"What do you want?" he asked the dark.

A scuttling sound answered. It was behind the clothes, beneath them, then suddenly against the back wall, scurrying up. He still couldn't see it, but he sensed it, the venomous repugnant thing.

"Justin," he whispered. "Can you see it?"

Justin lifted his head, his eyes red, his face so pale it glowed. Slowly, his gaze moved up to the ceiling and a dry, pained gasp came out of him. The Reaper followed

40

his gaze, and saw a flash of bloody pulp, teeth, fingers bent like claws. It made a sound he felt down to the soles of his human feet and launched itself at him. Instinctively, the Reaper turned and curved his body around the terrified child, protecting him. Something sliced the back of his neck and the bone-cold of death went through him.

It was over in a second. When he looked again, the closet was still; the presence gone. The boy's hot tears dampened his shirt.

"Shhhh, Justin. It's over."

Justin shook his head violently. "She'll come back."

She would. That brief encounter had told him enough. The thing that had crawled the walls of Justin's closet smelled of evil. Cold, focused evil. It was dead, yet there was something holding it here. Or something *it* had latched onto. The boy? The Reaper's arms clenched around the small body he held.

If it thought it could prey on this innocent child, it thought wrong.

"Don't worry about what you saw," he said softly. "It will have to go through me to get to you."

"But I don't want it to hurt you either," Justin whispered.

The Reaper smiled. "That's not going to happen."

Justin stared at him with troubled eyes and the Reaper felt as if he'd been weighed and measured by the time Justin finished.

"Okay," the boy said solemnly. "But don't tell Mom."

The Reaper frowned uncertainly.   He'd made this mistake already with the *Mom* word.

"Maggie," Justin clarified.  "Don't tell her."

"Why?"

"She'll be scared."

"I won't tell her, then."

"Promise?"

With all the dignity it was due, the Reaper promised.

"I believe you," Justin whispered.

With the child's scrawny arms around his neck, The Reaper carried Sam's son back downstairs.

# CHAPTER SEVEN

MAGGIE HAD SLEPT for all of two minutes. Sam filled her mind when she was awake and when she dozed . . . Sam filled her dreams. She gave up at six and climbed out of bed. Exhausted, she showered, styled her hair and applied her makeup with a heavy hand, hoping to hide the shadows under her eyes. She didn't want the kids to think she'd turned into a zombie while they'd slept.

Finally, she pulled on a pair of exercise pants and a t-shirt and with a deep breath, she stepped out of the room.

Justin's bedroom was just across the hall and she glanced at it automatically as she went by. The door stood wide open instead of cracked as she'd left it. It was too early for him to be awake, let alone out of his room. Surprised, she turned back and looked in. Justin wasn't in bed. With a frown, she entered, circling to the other side of the bed to make sure he hadn't rolled onto the floor in his sleep. That's when she noticed the open closet door. She paused, while unease filled her. Like all children, Justin considered the closet a breeding ground for monsters. It had been shut when she'd read him his story. It had been shut when she'd turned out the light. He would have reminded her if it hadn't been.

Frowning, she peered inside. All his small clothes hung in an orderly fashion, but there were gaps in between the hangers, like someone had shoved them apart. A dark, disturbing odor permeated the air. What *was* that?

She backed away, deciding it was high time the closet was cleaned, mentally adding it to the to-do list for this afternoon. In the hall, she checked the bathroom and headed for the stairs just as Lexi's door opened and her sleepy stepdaughter shuffled out of her room. Still in her pajamas with her hair mussed and her face scrubbed, she looked like the eleven year old child she was. She glanced at Maggie without the usual hostility in her eyes. Not awake enough for that.

"What's wrong?" she said.

"Justin didn't climb in bed with you last night, did he?"

Lexi shook her head.

Tamping down the ridiculous disquiet that inched in, Maggie hurried down the stairs. Lexi followed.

Halfway down, she saw Sam lying on the couch, bare-chested with the blankets bunched at his waist. Justin was curled against him, held safe in his arms, and the cat was snuggled at their feet. All three were sound asleep. Maggie froze, too shocked to take another step.

Right behind her, Lexi let out a soft, startled laugh. "What's that about? Did you sexile the dear husband on his first night home?"

Maggie gave Lexi a look over her shoulder and the girl flushed. The two of them had clear boundaries.

Maggie understood that Lexi didn't like her and Lexi understood that Maggie might tolerate her dislike, but never her disrespect. Lexi also knew that if she drove Maggie out, she'd be stuck with her father, her mother, or foster care. She was usually better at toeing the line.

Besides, Sam hadn't slept in this house for over nine months, let alone have a sexual relationship with her.

"Sorry," Lexi muttered.

"What's Justin doing down here?" Maggie asked, more to herself than Lexi.

"Why'd dad let him stay?" Lexi answered.

It was a good question. She and Lexi stared at each other with baffled expressions.

"He used to do things like that," Lexi went on, softly. Sadly. "He used to love us."

Maggie wanted to say, *He still loves you,* but she couldn't bring herself to add more lies to the ones Lexi had already endured. Instead, she dared to touch her stepdaughter and squeeze her hand.

"Everything changed when he married you," Lexi said, the moment gone.

"I know," Maggie answered. Lexi had told her as much many times over.

On the couch, Sam shifted. A second later, his long lashes lifted and he looked up, pinning Maggie with slumberous blue eyes. She frowned—mainly because she didn't want to swoon—and came the rest of the way down the stairs. Lexi turned abruptly and went back up.

Neither spoke as she descended, but Sam's heated gaze moved over her legs, her hips, lingering on her

45

breasts, then her mouth. Finally, he met her eyes. "Good morning," he said.

She was already fighting the effects of that possessive gleam but the low, husky voice nearly did her in.

"How did Justin get down here?" she whispered.

"Bad dream."

Usually, he crawled in bed with Maggie when that happened, but she'd closed her door last night. She swallowed the jarring notes of jealousy and guilt that played on her overwrought senses.

"What's wrong?" Sam asked, still prone. Still all-male, long, lean and sexy.

"Nothing," she answered softly, staring at him while emotions churned inside her, making it hard to catch her breath.

"I . . . ." She shook her head.

"You okay?" he murmured.

"I . . . I guess I'm just wondering . . .?"

He waited, brows up, tense. She could see it in the bunched muscles of his bare chest, the hard line of his jaw.

"*Who* is this man sleeping on my sofa?" she murmured. "That's what I wonder."

For a moment he simply stared back, not answering though there was a clear response in his eyes, if only she could decipher it. Finally, he swung his legs to the floor and sat. Justin popped up beside him, instantly wide awake.

"Our sofa," Sam said.

"What?" she asked, still trapped in that blue gaze. It made her dizzy, what she saw there, what she knew better than to believe.

"He means the sofa belongs to both of you," Justin offered helpfully.

"Thanks, buddy," Sam replied.

Justin turned *you're welcome* eyes on Maggie, as if he'd just solved a bigger mystery that she should thank him for, too. At last, she broke free of Sam's hypnotic hold.

"Time to get ready for school, Jus."

Justin hopped down, startling Minnie who unfurled from the foot of the couch. Sam shot the cat a disgusted, incredulous look.

"You," he said.

Minnie stretched sensationally, gave Sam a cool yowl, and sauntered off.

"When did we get that cat?" Sam asked in a dark voice.

"After you left. Don't take her attitude personally. Minnie hates everyone."

"Just like Lexi," Justin said.

"I don't hate everyone," Lexi piped in, coming down the stairs dressed in tight jeans and a t-shirt, eyes lined in bright blue with a clumsy hand. "Just you, dingus."

Sighing, Maggie headed for the kitchen.

# Chapter Eight

FOR THE REAPER, the next five days went much like the first. To his disappointment, the ghost hadn't reappeared so he'd had no chance to learn more about who "she" was. After Maggie cleaned the closet, Justin returned to his room. He didn't have much of a choice—he knew Maggie would have questioned it if he'd refused and the little man didn't want to worry her. He managed to hide his reluctance from everyone else, but before he went back to his room the first night, he hugged the Reaper and whispered, "You promise you won't let her get me, Dad?"

Justin's earnest use of *Dad* still brought a hard knot to a place beneath his breast bone. He wanted to swear to this child that no one—*nothing*—would ever harm him again. But by the very act of being there, an imposter father with goals that were far from altruistic, the Reaper was hurting Justin.

And when the time came for the Reaper to take Sam Sloan and return to the Beyond . . . what then? Who would stand between Justin and danger when the Reaper was gone? The child would be devastated over being abandoned again. Lexi, too, although to a smaller degree. She'd never let him in.

And Maggie . . . . What would she feel when he left her?

"I won't let it get you, Justin," he said gravely, feeling like he'd fallen into a pit of quicksand he couldn't escape. Each nuance of this human façade pulled him deeper. He still didn't have answers and with every passing hour, it became easier to think of himself as Sam. Not the Reaper . . . Sam. Sometimes he did it without even realizing.

If he didn't get out of this body soon, he never would. Worse, he feared he wouldn't *want* to. Maggie was an irresistible enticement, but the children . . . the unit they made as a family . . . it filled something inside him that he hadn't known he lacked.

He was still relegated to the couch at night, but that didn't really matter. He spent the long hours of dark awake, patrolling the house, making sure everyone under his care was safe.

The irony of that did not escape him.

When he did finally sleep, he awakened with a stiff neck and a yearning so deep he could barely contain it. He didn't understand the changes at work within him, but even reapers were sentient enough to recognize that a metamorphosis had taken place. He'd never be the same.

So far, he'd seen no sign that he was missed in the Beyond, though he waited, expecting harsh, unrelenting retaliation at any moment. By fault or accident, he'd broken the most important law of the Beyond: No mixing with humans. Most humans had never even heard of the Beyond. Those that had, mistook it for heaven . . . or hell, depending on their perspective. They didn't understand that it was a world, whole unto itself. It was both of those things and, at the same time, it was neither.

He wasn't the first to break the laws of the Beyond, though. He'd heard rumors of another Reaper who'd taken things a step too far and stolen a body for his own purposes. Until now, he hadn't understood how that could happen. If it was true, he could only surmise that it had ended badly. He expected the same cruel result for himself, even though he was a prisoner in this body, not a thief. Retribution from the Beyond was dealt in black and white. Shades of gray didn't matter.

But deep down, he had no regrets. In the small amount of time since he'd opened his eyes in this human body, he'd experienced a spectrum of emotion that had illuminated his world. He didn't like half of the feelings that kept him occupied—the inexplicable angst whenever Maggie walked by and he couldn't touch her; the bewildering need to make her smile; the endless longing to hold her against him; the frustration of not knowing what would happen if she let him.

He understood the mechanics of copulation. He'd reaped men and women in the throes of passion countless times. But now he knew on a cellular, *human* level, the experience would be entirely different from this side of the equation. In this world, everything came layered in complexity and sentiments.

This body yearned to mate with Maggie, but he knew she would require an emotional connection that Sam—the Reaper—*who or whatever he'd become*—feared he'd be unable to make.

What if she found him lacking? What if he couldn't live up to the expectation her human husband had set?

He probed that hollow place that housed the remnants of Sam Sloan and found what he always did, echoes of incomplete memory. His childhood was there in chips and splinters. A smiling mother who smelled of soap and, inexplicably, apples. A doting father who'd had more muscle than brain. There'd been a sister at one time, but she'd died in a car crash when she was twenty-eight. Sam had met his first wife, Janet, at the funeral.

And there the memories dried up in the drought-stricken land of Sam's psyche. He couldn't even picture his ex-wife's face. He didn't remember the birth of their children, the divorce that had left them in his custody, or the years that came after.

But he remembered meeting Maggie that day in front of the coffee shop.

*Maggie* . . . .

As if summoned she walked through the front door, dressed in clingy pants that lovingly hugged every curve and a loose top that hung to her hips. Sneakers covered her feet and all that gorgeous hair had been pulled back in a ponytail that bobbed with each step. She'd just taken Justin to the bus stop and her cheeks were flushed from her walk. She had more makeup on than usual. Was she hiding sleepless nights beneath her mask?

He finished his lazy inspection at her eyes. Humans called it the window to the soul. He believed it, looking into hers, but he wondered what she saw as she gazed back. Did she suspect his soul was borrowed?

He followed her into the kitchen, remembering how it felt to hold her in his arms. "What are you thinking?" he asked.

"The same thing I'm always thinking," she answered, making herself a cup of coffee. "That I'm stuck in some bizarre hiatus. I don't have a clue what happens next."

"What do you want to happen?" he asked.

She sighed and took a sip of coffee, glancing at him from beneath her lashes. "I don't know. Maybe I just want things to make sense."

"Things? You mean like me?" he asked warily.

"And me." She lifted one shoulder and tilted her head. "Do you know . . . when you asked me to marry you, I couldn't say yes fast enough."

"Why?"

She raised her brows, and he realized the question probably sounded strange to her. Presumably, she'd fallen in love, that's why.

"You're a beautiful woman, Maggie. I can't believe he—I'm the only man who's noticed."

"Why do you do that? Refer to yourself in third person?"

His face grew hot as he tried to come up with a reasonable explanation. "Maybe I feel disconnected from who I am."

"And who is that? Because you're not the same man who left."

In ways she couldn't even imagine, but he certainly didn't want to take her down that path. She didn't know the truth and no guess in the world would bring her to it. "What about the man you couldn't wait to marry?"

She shook her head. "You're not him either. I don't know who you are."

She looked lost and sad. He'd put that sorrow in her eyes and he wished he knew how to take it away. Gently, Sam—the Reaper, he corrected himself anxiously—took her shoulders between his hands. Surprised, her gaze rose to meet his as her hands came up to his chest. She meant to push him away, but the pressure eased after a moment and her fingers just rested there.

"Tell me about us," he murmured.

"Why do you keep asking that? Don't you want to know other things?"

"Like?"

"What you do for a living? If your father is still alive—"

"No. I only want to know about you and me."

"Okay," she said, drawing it out. "What should I tell you?"

"Everything. How did I win you?"

A small smile curled her lips. "I'm not a prize."

He could argue that, but didn't see the point. Already he'd discerned that Maggie didn't know just how beautiful she was.

"You didn't have to do much," she said softly. "After we met—"

"Collided."

Another almost-smile. "After that, we just stood there and talked. You bought me another cup of coffee and we talked some more. For hours. I gave you my phone number, you called me that night and I . . . ." She laughed softly. "I became addicted to you. I'd say I was obsessed, but it went both ways. At least, I thought it did."

"At the hospital, you said you weren't surprised to see me there. Why?"

She blushed. His face was close to hers and he could almost feel the heat.

"I said a lot of things I shouldn't have. I'm sorry, Sam."

"I'm sorry, too," he murmured. "For all of the things I can't remember doing. I must have been insane to leave you."

But even as he said it, he realized a reason for that insanity had begun to surface in his mind. It was shadowed and vague, and yet it felt right. A threat had come to this house. According to Justin, it began the night before Sam had come home. What if it had been here before? What if Sam had left to draw it away?

She met his eyes, hers wide and hurt. "Why did you ask for me?" she whispered.

It took him a moment to follow. "You mean at the hospital?"

She nodded. "I hadn't heard from you in months. Not that I'm complaining about that, but suddenly you're back, with a *gunshot* wound, and asking for me. Being nice to me. And I keep waiting for the punch line, Sam. I know I can't keep punishing you for something you don't even remember, but I can't pretend this is real. You could wake up tomorrow, remember everything, and leave me all over again."

"That's not going to happen, Maggie," he said, that knot back under his breastbone.

"How do you know?"

"Because you're right. I'm not the same man. Not anymore."

She was shaking her head, eyes glittering with unshed tears. "Since the moment I saw you again, all of these blasted feelings keep rising up. And then you didn't die and—"

"Sorry about that."

"That's not what I meant."

"You sure?"

She sighed and her head fell forward. "I don't even know anymore, Sam. I look in your eyes and I see . . . ."

*What? What did she see?*

"A stranger."

"I get that," he said softly, shifting just a little more. Bringing her closer inch by inch. "I feel a little split in two, myself. But maybe that's how it needs to be. I can't undo what's done. But I can be here for you now."

"See . . . " she began with a headshake, "all those words sound right, but you're asking for a leap of faith that I can't take. You came into my life like a whirlwind, then you left the same way. I've spent the last year just trying to put the pieces back together and now here you are, and I feel like I got it all wrong."

"You deserve answers, Maggie. I know you do. I'm not asking you to just forget everything that happened in the past, but I'm telling you, somewhere deep inside me, I know it wasn't a random thing. I left for a reason. And some instinct I can't even identify is telling me that I did it to protect you."

He rested his forehead against hers. The smell of her skin filled him with calm while at the same time, it woke up his senses, making him want to taste. "Tell me about us, Maggie," he said softly. "Help me remember what changed me."

"I don't know if I can. We married so fast—"

"Why?"

"Because waiting seemed redundant. I'd never felt anything like it before. You made me feel wanted—not just physically," she said, glancing up and quickly away, but not before he saw the heat in her eyes. "There was that, though. We were good together in . . . you know."

Not as much as he wanted to, but he let her go on at her own pace, content for the moment to be so near. To touch her.

"You let me be a part of your family," she said softly.

"What about your family?"

"My parents died when I was young. We'd never been that close, though. They were both academics. My dad studied ancient civilizations and my mother, women's issues. They traveled all over the world. Sometimes they took me, but even then they were off to their presentations and faculty socials. Even when I was with them, they left me behind."

He heard the soft hitch in her voice and understood things she didn't say. He'd wondered why such a young and beautiful woman would have given herself so freely to a man saddled with two children and a crazy ex-wife. Now he knew. Sam had included her. Or so she'd thought . . . . His leaving must have felt like the ultimate betrayal.

"I loved them," she said, almost defensively. As if he'd insisted otherwise.

"I know."

"I didn't realize I had so many abandonment issues, until you. First you made me feel whole. Then you ripped me apart." She looked up at him. Into him.

"I don't want to be a stranger anymore, Maggie."

"You think it's that easy?"

"It could be."

He stared into her eyes, watching them widen. She licked her lips nervously and caught her breath as a soft groan escaped him. Waiting for her to push him away, he slid his hands down her shoulders and around to her back. Instead, she stood very still, hardly breathing. He was aware of the quiet house, the hours they had until the children would be home from school.

"I died that day in the hospital," he said, remembering those moments after the Reaper and the human had merged and their heart had stopped beating. Even now, it made him shudder to remember the absolute darkness that enveloped them.

"I know," she whispered. "The doctors told me that they'd brought you back."

He nodded, that hard lump of emotions inside swelling. He should walk away, now, before he did more damage than he already had. But she smelled so sweet, felt so good, and his need for her had become so great.

Now that he stood on the edge of what he wanted, though, he could see clearly to the other side. How could this end, but badly? Maggie had endured too much already.

"I'm sorry," he said, uncertain if he was apologizing for what he meant to do or what he'd already done.

"Don't be," she said. "It's not . . . you're different, now, and I'm still trying to figure it all out. But the first words you spoke were for me and I can't forget that. If you tell me you meant it, that this isn't some game . . . ."

He could hardly breathe, hardly think, but she didn't require either. She needed a pledge, a promise, and he wanted her to have it so badly that he found the words on his lips, refusing to be held back.

"It's not a game, Maggie."

She shook her head, but her gaze had fixed on his mouth and he took the chance before she changed her mind. Her lips were soft and silky. Against his, they felt like nothing he'd imagined and everything he'd imagined. The memories of this in Sam's banks were generic, not of Maggie specifically. He was glad for that. He wanted this experience for his own. Sensations shot through him in sharp, hot waves, a torrent of passion and lightning.

She made a soft sound of surrender in her throat, murmured something that might have been, *I'm a fool,* and she kissed him back.

The feel of her; the smell of her, the sweet intoxicating scent . . . . All of it filled him, pushed out the vestiges of the man Sam had been, overwhelmed the foundation of the Reaper inside, and forced them both into the moment that was now. Here. *Her.* Him.

Maggie tugged at his shirt, pulling it free of his jeans, then took his hand, leading him up the stairs and into the bedroom she'd banned him from. The door closed behind them. She locked it.

"I've been thinking about this since I opened my eyes," he said, that hint of accent that only appeared at rare times adding a husky rasp to his voice. "Since I came to life."

There were more words he should say, but the swamp of emotion made speaking an impossible feat. The Reaper felt clumsy, the man felt hungry . . . and the place somewhere in the middle, exposed. She stared into his eyes, hers a jaded green so raw, so vulnerable, that he didn't dare hesitate.

Like he understood the feelings welling up inside him or the instinct to claim her in some human, *male* way, he took her face in his hands and kissed her. She kissed him back, her hands moving beneath his shirt, pushing it up until he let her go, but only long enough to strip it off.

Her eyes had turned into a stormy sea and a pulse beat hard at her throat as she stared at his bare chest with a hunger that threatened to consume them both. His hands felt big and clumsy as he gently pulled her shirt over her head and tossed it to the side. Her skin was as smooth, indescribably warm, and flawlessly beautiful. A bra the same shade as her skin held her breasts in an embrace of lace and satin. He touched one gently, groaning at the weight, the softness he'd only imagined before. He bent his head and covered it with his mouth, needing to know the taste and feel, letting the lace rasp against his tongue, acting on instinct he couldn't have denied if he'd tried.

"Take it off," he murmured, his voice so deep it throbbed against the quiet.

She arched back, hands meeting between her shoulder blades as she unfastened the bra and shrugged it off. The stretchy pants came next without him even asking. She stood before him in pale, silky panties and his body went up in flames.

He'd never imagined that just looking at someone could make him feel so many things. He was overwhelmed by this gift she offered him, by the freedom to touch, to take . . . to give. He didn't know where to start or how to proceed, but his body understood every nuance of her invitation.

He lifted her up and turned her, laying her out on the bed so he could follow her down to the soft mattress. Her body yielded to his and the perfection in the feeling wrenched another groan from him. He kissed her deeply, trying to slow his racing his heart. Trying to experience each second . . . trying to slow down when every tightened nerve begged for him to rush.

She was gloriously naked and in his arms, where he felt she'd always belonged. But fear suddenly crept in. He'd never done this before and though he'd managed to toe the line between human and Reaper, he knew in a deep place that had been growing since the moment he'd opened his eyes, the time had come for him to decide

Reaper or human? He couldn't be both.

One came without the heavy burden of emotion, of mortality, of humanity.

The other came with Maggie.

"Sam?" she murmured.

"Say my name again," he whispered against her lips, into her mouth. And when she spoke his name, he took it inside and made it his own.

With the acceptance of this human name came a rush of instinct that washed over him, as old as the tide, as real as the woman he held.

From this moment on, there was no turning back. He would fight the Beyond if they came for him. The old Sam had become a fading pulse inside him that wouldn't survive on its own, but the new Sam combined them both and was strong, able. He would use that strength to protect the things Sam had loved. Only death would take him away.

Maggie need never know what he was or what he'd been, not when the lie would keep her safe. Not when the truth might turn her away from him.

His expression must have conveyed at least some of what he was thinking, though there was no way Maggie could truly understand what it meant. She stared at him with those big eyes, and he kissed her again to dispel the concern that had suddenly appeared.

He trailed his hands over her body, imbued by commitment if not experience, and she flexed languidly, bowing to the force of his passion. He felt her beneath the skin, in his blood stream, to the bone. With long, lazy kisses, he worked his way down her body, learning her like an intricate language he longed to speak. She made a sound of anticipation when he reached her hip bone, the soft belly between them, the apex of her thighs.

"I'm not . . . I don't think . . . ."

Whatever she wasn't, whatever she didn't think, became a whisper as he sealed his mouth over her sex, losing himself in the intimacy of kissing her just there. Of the way her body went boneless and her fingers clenched the covers, her feet arching to tip-toe. He kissed and sucked and lost himself in her sounds and scent, ignoring his own body as he tuned into hers. High, breathless sounds came from her lips. She rose up on elbows, watching him as he learned her body.

"Oh," she said when he sealed his lips over her again. "*Oh.*"

He felt the storm building within her . . . the tension and heat of it. She came with a soft shout that stiffened every muscle in both of their bodies. He rode the orgasm with her, feeling it crank his own excitement into something wondrous and painful.

He'd never known, never imagined that pleasing another could change him, but it had. Already, he felt different, more human than he'd thought possible. When the last wave went through her, he moved up.

In a moment, his pants were open, off, and he was braced between her spread legs. Poised above her body, he stared into her eyes, understanding that in taking what she offered, he'd be giving away pieces of himself, pieces he might never regain. It didn't matter. Maggie already owned his heart.

Kissing her again, he pushed slowly, deeply inside her, reeling from the sensations. The hot, tight fit, the feeling of coming home. Nothing he'd experienced so far could compare to this. He died, just a little, in the pure pleasure of it.

She gazed into his eyes as he buried himself in her body. That steady stare stripped him down while the heat of her, the soft curves of breasts and hips, reconstructed the man he would be. He thrust deep, setting a pace she matched with her hips. He watched her, feeling his way to pleasing her. The sounds she made . . . the way her brow puckered between her eyes . . . the look of passion in her heavy-lidded eyes . . . .

He moved lower and caught one nipple between his teeth, nipping just hard enough to make her body bow, listening for the rewarding gasp as her hand curled at the back of his neck, urging him to do it again. Her hand slid down her body and her fingers went to the point at the apex of her thighs where she was most feminine, most sensitive. He watched and learned, then replaced her fingers with his. Bracing one hand over her shoulder, he raised up and added the seduction of his touch to the dominance of his thrusts.

He felt the tightness of her again and nothing existed in the world but the need to hold her, possess her, make her cry his name. She clenched around him and came in a hot rush that reverberated through him like thunder. It took all his control to hold on as she rocked her pelvis into his, but that small, aggressive surrender destroyed him. Something had broken apart inside him, leaving him shattered as he climbed to a peak he could barely fathom. What pieces would be left when he reached the top? In a rush of heat and passion, he shot over the edge and into a climax that transformed man and Reaper, resurrecting him as a new creation, one that combined their two worlds and made them one.

After a long moment, Sam and Maggie collapsed, holding one another tight as the afternoon sun spilled through the window.

Sam—no longer the Reaper—kissed her once more, hoping to slake his thirst for her. Knowing it would take more than one time. He was still deep inside her body, and even that wasn't close enough.

# CHAPTER NINE

MAGGIE LAY IN Sam's arms, boneless, happy . . . and confused. After all the months of putting herself back together again, it had taken him so little time to break her down. She didn't know whether to run for the hills or hold on tight.

"What are you thinking?" he asked, his mouth against her throat, his hands soft over her body.

"That I must be insane."

He cupped her face and kissed her gently. "I want to be your husband, Maggie. That's all I want. Please let me."

A small laugh bubbled out. All the words he spoke were exactly the ones she needed to hear. Pieces of her heart that had shriveled and waned over the past year now burst into new life. She had no defense against the hope in heart or the charm Sam exuded. She could only hope he wouldn't make her regret this moment.

"I shouldn't make this so easy for you," she grumbled.

"What part of this was easy?" he teased. "I thought I was going to have to die again to get you here."

His kiss both rewarded her capitulation and punished

her for her uncertainty.

"I'm glad you came home, Sam," she whispered.

His blue eyes darkened and a soft smile curved his beautiful lips. "I'm glad you're glad," he murmured in a voice so low it tingled along her nerves.

She cleared her throat. "You know you're going to have to work to make your daughter happy about it though . . . right?"

"I know it will take time with Lexi," he agreed. "But I'm not going anywhere."

"You sure about that, Sam? Because I hear something in your voice that sounds like doubt."

It took a moment for him to meet her eyes. When she saw his, she knew why.

"I don't know where I've been, Maggie. Maybe that scares me."

And there lie the crux of her fears, the storm on her horizon. Neither one of them knew where he'd been or what he'd been doing. And it scared her, too, but he looked so sincere, so troubled and earnest that all she could say was, "We'll figure it out, Sam. We'll figure it out together."

She didn't want to think of that, not now. Not while she was in his arms and feeling hopeful for the first time in forever.

His head lowered and she tipped hers back to meet his lingering kiss. She was falling all over again and there wasn't a damned thing she could do to stop it.

Sam had always been a conscientious lover. He'd always put thought and consideration into making love, but it wasn't until now that she realized . . . there'd been no feeling.

Making love with this new version of Sam . . . it was *all* feeling. Raw, emotional, sometimes clumsy, sometimes rough. His touch lacked the slick confidence the old Sam had worn like a shield. In its place was passion . . . fire . . . hunger. He'd made her feel desired, like touching and tasting her was more important than breathing.

Which was exactly how she felt about him.

She couldn't stop burying her face against his chest, his throat, the hollow of his shoulder. His scent was like Maggie catnip and she couldn't get enough of it. She rubbed against him, smiling with satisfaction as he groaned and his arms tightened around her.

He gave a sharp hiss as she kissed her way down the ridged muscles of his abdomen, nipping at the flesh in the sloped musculature of his hips.

She took him in her mouth all at once, as much as she could, and Sam made another sound that fired all of her senses and made her want to drive him over the edge into oblivion, as he'd done to her. It made her dizzy, this power she seemed to have . . . this power she'd never had before. It made her fierce.

His muscles clenched, thighs tight against her shoulders, long legs bracketing her body. Her hands were jealous of her lips and they joined in the sensual play, stroking him while she sealed her mouth over the silky flesh and sucked.

"Jesus, God," he breathed, hands in her hair, gentle

against her scalp.

She pulled her knees up under her so she could touch him everywhere. His breath came in deep, harsh draws. His hips came up off the bed, flexing at her erotic torture. Finally, he cursed softly and pulled her up to straddle him. She held him and lowered her body until he was seated as deep as he could go.

Neither one of them seemed to be breathing. Maggie wasn't even sure she ever would again.

"Okay?" he asked, one hand flat on her belly, the other an anchor at her hip.

"Yeah," she answered.

They moved like dancers and she fit him like a glove—she always had. But the way he responded, his eyes on hers, watching for clues to what she liked, what she needed . . . that was disconcertingly new. His thumb slipped down to circle the tight ball of nerves that needed his attention and Maggie gasped with pleasure.

He pumped hard and fast, slow and languid, watching her all the while. She was so into him that each shift of muscle reverberated through her. Her knees stretched wider and he grasped her hips, helping her up as he thrust deep and long.

"Fuck," he breathed, the crude word dark on his tongue. "I didn't . . . ."

She'd never know what he didn't, because thinking, speaking, became impossible endeavors. All she knew was his body, his touch and the heat of him inside her. He sat up, rolling her beneath him as he made love to her like it was the first time. Like every time with her would be a first.

Arm braced over her head, free hand at work between their bodies, he drove her to a point beyond herself, to another version of who she could be. He lowered his face, his nose beside hers, mouth open. Hers, too. Their breath pooled between them, an aphrodisiac that she mainlined.

The tension built inside her, inside him. She felt his muscles harden, his thighs flex. His fingers moved faster and Maggie came with a soft cry as he rode her hard, while her muscles clenched and waves of hot release went through her. A moment later, he shouted her name and came with her, wreaking havoc on her senses, destroying the last vestiges of her will to ever resist him.

# CHAPTER TEN

AS MAGGIE LOADED the dishwasher with their dinner dishes, it was hard to pretend that she hadn't spent the day in bed with Sam . . . her *husband*. But Maggie wasn't ready for the kids to know about the shift in her relationship with him. She wasn't sure what the shift even meant for them. They both knew that if—*when*—Sam's memory returned, everything might reset. Deep down, she expected it. Waited for it. Dreaded it.

Yet he seemed so certain that wouldn't happen, and Maggie wanted it to be true so badly.

But that had been the problem all along, hadn't it? She'd always tried to make Sam into what she wanted, which wasn't the same thing as what he was.

The kids' world had already been turned upside down, though. It wouldn't hurt to keep things quiet for a little while, at least until Sam was fully healed. There was a good chance his memory would never return— that's what the doctors said. Maggie didn't know which outcome she hoped for. If he got his memory back, he might remember why he'd left and do it again. If he didn't, she'd be waiting, never able to trust what she had.

Sighing, she rinsed the last plate and set it in the

machine with the others. Sam wiped down the table, making room for the kids to do their homework. From the outside in, they looked like the perfect American family. Something she wanted desperately.

After he finished, Sam leaned against the counter, watching her with those heartbreaker eyes, starting a slide show of their afternoon in her head. How she could still be turned on and wanting him when they'd spent so many hours in bed was beyond her.

The kids took their seats at the table and started their homework, talking occasionally. Maggie was still getting used to that. Before Sam had come home, Lexi had always confined herself to her room except for the few minutes required to eat, clear her dishes, and leave again. Maybe her father wouldn't have such a long road in winning over his daughter after all. Maybe the fairy tale could come true.

She had a bottle of wine on the bottom shelf of the fridge. She took it out and stood with the bottle in her hand while her thoughts hijacked her motor functions. Silently, Sam took it from her.

"Would you like me to open this?"

She wasn't used to anyone *doing* for her, but mutely she nodded.

Both kids looked up. Without a word, Lexi went to a drawer and pulled out the opener. Justin did an adorable mime of how Sam should proceed, just in case his memory failed him there, too.

In the dark months before Sam had moved out, moved on, he and his son hadn't really resembled one

71

another. That had changed, too. Maggie wasn't certain if Justin had matured or if Sam had softened, but now the two looked so much alike that it made her heart hurt.

The doorbell rang just as Sam handed her a glass of cold Pinot Grigio. All four of them looked up, as if doorbells were portents of doom. Sam set the bottle down and went to answer it. She and the kids gathered in the arched doorway so they could see.

His big body and broad shoulders blocked their view at first, but when he stepped back they all saw the two men on the porch. Maggie recognized the detectives who'd questioned him in the hospital and dread filled her stomach. Sam's expression was grim as he invited them in, and they took seats in the living room. Like small moons, the children followed. A moment later, so did Maggie.

Justin perched on the arm of Sam's chair and Sam's hand went to the boy's waist, keeping him balanced. She and Lexi exchanged a glance before they settled on the loveseat to Sam's right.

The officers seemed uncomfortable with their audience. Both were older men, obviously veterans who'd seen it all. They shared a look around their eyes that labeled them law, but one was slight and sharp-featured, while the other had a bulldog appearance, right down to his paunch.

"Sorry to disturb you at dinner time," the smaller of the two—Detective Hartman—said. "We have some new information that's led to more questions."

Sam nodded as the bigger man—Maggie couldn't

remember his name—opened a leather notebook he'd brought in. Once again, they looked at the children and Maggie.

"Is there somewhere we can speak alone?" Bulldog asked Sam.

"Why?" Maggie wanted to know.

"We don't want to upset the children," Hartman answered.

Lexi snorted disrespectfully. When all eyes turned her way, she blushed. "Come on, Jus. Let's finish our homework."

Surprised by her compliance, Maggie watched them return to the kitchen table. They'd still be able to hear everything, but the distance seemed to satisfy the detectives. Sam caught her eye as she turned around. He looked worried. He'd worn that expression when the detectives had come to the hospital, too, but she wasn't sure if it was rooted in his amnesia or just the opposite.

"When was the last time you saw your ex-wife, Sam?" Hartman asked.

"I don't know," he answered flatly.

Both detectives gave him an unwavering look. Waiting him out. That's what they did on CSI, and it usually worked. But Sam only answered their silence with more.

"We have a witness that places you at her house two days before you were shot," Bulldog said.

Sam swallowed hard and shook his head. His brows had pulled tight with frustration.

"Why are you asking about Janet?" Maggie said.

"Because no one's seen her since. A neighbor called in when her dog wouldn't shut up. Animal control found the dog chained up and the house ransacked. They notified us."

The quiet following that declaration seemed to echo all around them. Maggie felt sick to her stomach. Worried, she glanced over her shoulder. Lexi and Justin had moved to the archway. They stared back with bleak expressions.

"Is the dog okay?" Justin asked.

Detective Bulldog nodded and the hard line of his mouth softened. "The dog's fine. Your mom's neighbor took it in."

"She's not my mom," Justin said in a low, vehement voice.

The detective blinked, before turning suspicious eyes back on Sam. "Who shot you, Sam?" he asked abruptly.

Sam wore the distant expression he got when he was scanning his inner thoughts. Finally, he shook his head again. "I still don't remember." He covered his face with his open hands, frustration in every line of his body. "I can't remember a damned thing before the hospital. I mean, I can remember growing up. My sister's funeral. After that . . . nothing except meeting Maggie."

"That was after your divorce to Janet Sloan?" Bulldog asked, a sharp note of interrogation in the query.

"Yes."

"You remember that?"

"No. Maggie told me."

She had, earlier when he'd asked more questions

about their past.

"Any idea why you might have been visiting your ex two weeks ago?"

"No, but every time I think of her, I get a knot in my gut. From what I hear, there's a reason for that."

"She's crazy," Lexi said.

Hartman nodded. "We know that she was institutionalized for a time. We're trying to get access to those records."

"She set our house on fire," Justin declared.

"You don't even remember," Lexi said.

"I do, too."

Lexi rolled her eyes. "He was just a baby."

"Does your mother stay in touch?" Hartman asked. Apparently, they'd given up on isolating the children from the conversation.

"She's not our mother," Justin repeated angrily.

"Egg donor," Lexi clarified. "And no."

Both detectives looked at Maggie. "You've been married to Sam for about a year?"

Maggie nodded. Her mouth was dry.

"Did you ever meet his ex-wife?"

"Just once, right after Sam and I got married."

"She never came to the house to see her children? Never visited?"

Maggie shook her head. "My understanding is that the courts found her a danger, and she's only allowed to see the kids under supervision. She never made the effort."

"What about you?" Bulldog asked.

"What about her?" Sam responded, bristling.

"I only wondered if she'd ever tried to arrange a meeting. Children need to know their parents, good or bad."

"Do you have kids, Detective?" Maggie asked.

He shook his head. "But I have parents."

"And did either of them ever set your house on fire with you inside?"

He narrowed his eyes at her before turning to Sam. "Where were you when you were shot?" he asked, throwing them all off balance.

"The parking lot of my apartment," Sam answered automatically.

"You remember?"

Sam blinked, hope and dread battling in his expression. After a moment, he shook his head. "You told me, the first time you questioned me. I was shot somewhere between nine and eleven p.m."

"Why do you live in an apartment, Sam?" Hartman asked. "You have a lovely family that obviously cares about you."

Sam gave the detective a cold look. "My relationship with my family is not your business."

"It is when murder is involved."

"Murder?" Sam repeated. "Whose murder?"

"Possibly Janet Sloan's."

"Possibly? A moment ago, you said she was missing. You don't know that there's even been a murder, do you?" Sam said.

"This isn't my first rodeo. I may not have the facts to

76

back it up, but I'll get them."

"Sam," Maggie murmured, touching his arm. "You don't have to answer their questions. You haven't done anything wrong."

He looked at her fingers resting on his arm and covered them with his own. His hand was warm, his touch so familiar and, at the same time, so completely foreign.

"I'd answer them if I could," he said to her. Then, to the detectives. "I'll cooperate and answer any questions you have. Believe me, I'd like to know who put a bullet in my head, too. I want to make sure my family is safe."

Both detectives had squinty eyes as they assessed this statement. Did it ping against their lie meters? She had no way of knowing.

Lexi and Justin came in the room again. Justin resumed his place on the arm of the chair and Lexi came to stand on Sam's other side. They presented a unified front that brought a lump to Maggie's throat. With a deep breath, she moved behind Sam's chair, between the children. She put a hand on each of their shoulders. Lexi glanced up and met her eyes for a brief second. She didn't say anything, but she didn't move away.

The detectives noted it all. After a moment, they stood. Hartman handed Sam a card. "If you hear from your ex-wife, we'd like to know."

"Or if you remember anything at all," Bulldog tacked on. "Call us."

"I will," Sam said, standing as well. He shook their hands and escorted them out the door.

Maggie and the children remained where they were, listening, but the men spoke softly and they couldn't make out the words.

She wondered what the detectives were thinking. She wondered what she and the kids were thinking. Two weeks ago, they would have thought the worst, but in a very short time, Sam had turned the tables. Desperately, Maggie prayed for the best.

# CHAPTER ELEVEN

MAGGIE HAD ALWAYS enjoyed the moments before bedtime when Lexi occasionally shared some piece of her day and Justin would climb between the covers, excited for his story. Tonight it took too long and her awareness of Sam behind her was too overwhelming. How quickly he'd become the center of her world again.

He seemed distracted. Worried. After she turned on Justin's nightlight, she led him into her room and closed the door.

"Talk," she said.

He shot her a wary look. "Where do I start? It's like there's a wall in my head. I don't remember Janet—not even what she looks like."

"Would a picture help?" she asked, her stomach knotted. There had to be a reason why he didn't remember her, but that reason wouldn't be good and she feared it as much as she needed to hear it.

"Do you have one?" he said.

"No, but I think Lexi does. I'll ask her."

"Don't. Not tonight. She's already upset enough. I don't want to make it worse."

She stared at him, eyes misting. "I must be crazy."

"Why?"

"Because I'm starting to believe you, Sam. Believe *in you*. And I know that sooner or later you're going to make me regret it."

"Why are you so sure?"

"Because there's something in your eyes telling me that you're lying to me. Again. Still."

He sighed and looked at his feet. Avoiding her eyes?

"You're wrong," he said.

"Am I, Sam? Do you think I don't know what's going on? You think I can't feel it?"

"What are you talking about?"

Definitely wariness in his voice, now. She wanted to cry. She wanted to shake him until he told her what she wanted to hear.

But that wouldn't be the truth, would it?

"Yeah, you look like my husband. You even smell like him, God help me. But Sam was never as *considerate* as you are. He would have been knocking on Lexi's door, demanding a picture even if she was sound asleep."

"You want me to wake her up?"

"No, I want you to tell me who you really are."

"You know that, Maggie." He moved closer, touching her face. "I'm your husband."

She blinked at the tears blurring her vision. "You are not my husband. You may look like the man I married, but you aren't my husband."

"Then you tell me. Who am I?" he demanded.

"I don't know that either. But you are not my

husband."

"How do you know?"

"I just do."

"How, Maggie?"

"I just do."

"That's not good enough. How?"

"I know because . . . ."

"How, Maggie?"

She looked up. "He never touched me the way you do."

Sam stared at her, his lips silent over words they formed. Uncertainty glimmered in his eyes before his lashes came down to hide it. "I'm sorry. I don't remember how we—"

"I don't want you to remember that," she said, hindered by the giant lump in her throat that tried to silence her voice. She covered her face, not sure if she wanted to sob or shout. Both, probably.

"Hey," he said, pulling her hands away. "Talk to me. Please."

She sucked in a deep breath, tried to find her backbone, settled for a stiff upper lip. Inside, a well of grief and anger had been stewing, waiting for this moment to boil over. Pieces of her childhood floated at the top, alongside of chunks of her dreams and a peppering of her marriage. Now, she didn't know how to turn down the heat, how to let it all settle again.

She closed her eyes, trying to feel her way through this. Start at the beginning . . . that made sense.

"I was raised by . . . *distant* parents, Sam. My mother

and father didn't have me because they wanted children or a family. They were complete with just the two of them, but for whatever reason, they felt the need to procreate. I think I must have been a science experiment. Something they grew in a petri dish so they could document its stages."

She turned her back on him, but he didn't let her move away. He stood close behind her, wrapping those strong arms around her, sheltering her from the emotional mess inside her. She was too old to still be so devastated by her childhood, especially when hers had been better than most. She hadn't been used or abused. She'd only been ignored.

"I spent my whole life trying to be noticed. Seriously. Like a five year old at a birthday party. I tried it all. I was the best little girl, the worst teenager. I can relate to Lexi, because I was her. Hurt. Scorned. Lashing out. None of it helped. By the time I got to college, I was so needy that I couldn't even stand the sight of myself. I kept looking for love in all the wrong places." She laughed and covered her face again, past humiliations rolling into the moment.

"And then I met you. Successful. So handsome, I could hardly breathe. And interested in me. I realize now that I made you into the perfect man, even when you weren't. I wanted so badly to be a part of your world, your family, and when you invited me in . . . I went. Even when I doubted you . . . when I doubted myself. Even when some voice inside me said it was a mistake."

"You don't think I loved you?"

"In your own way, maybe. It wasn't until today when you made love to me, that I truly understood the difference . . . . It felt so new. It wasn't just physical, not with you. You *touched* me, Sam," she said, placing a hand over her heart. "Here. You never did that before, but I never let myself acknowledge it. I guess I didn't understand my own feelings about you . . . about me . . . not until now."

She pulled away and moved across the room. "In the past year, I've learned to be strong. I had to. I've learned to make my own way, my own happiness. I won't go back to seeing what I want to see instead of what's really there. So I'm asking you now, Sam. Tell me why when I look at you, I see the man I married. But when I look inside you . . . ." Her tears spilled over and trailed down her face. "Tell me why I see a different man looking out. One who wants to be known. One worthy of my love."

# CHAPTER TWELVE

IF SHE'D ASKED in any other way, he might have been able to resist, maintain the lie, stick with the plan. But as he stared at Maggie, his heart was so full that he thought it might break into a million pieces. So much for thinking he didn't have one.

She was right. He did want to be known. He'd thought he could live the lie, so long as it meant keeping Maggie and the kids safe. Making love to her had opened a new facet of life that he'd never even imagined. Now, it lay in front of him, a magical road he could only follow if he left the lies behind.

What she asked for though, would destroy her. Leave him alone on this path, watching the road to happiness wash away.

"You've asked me to trust you when everything that's happened tells me to turn away," she said in a low voice, her anguish tangible. "It's only fair that I ask you for the same thing."

The moment of truth had come and gone, leaving him on this jagged edge of reckoning. She'd never forgive what he'd done, what he'd taken without asking.

He'd had no choice when he'd been sucked into this

world against his will, yet his desire to touch her had been the catalyst. And once here, once he'd experienced what it really meant to touch, to hold . . . .

He'd selfishly let the charade play on.

He stared into her tearful face, and saw the punishment he deserved. She would banish him from this outlawed life and he would have no ground on which to take a stand. All he could hope for was a chance to eliminate the danger that surrounded her before he ended what he should never have begun.

"Sam died, Maggie," he said, his voice a broken thing that made him wince. "You know that."

She frowned at the way he said *Sam* instead of *I,* but nodded woodenly.

"And in death, there comes a way to the afterlife," he went on.

Her brows came together, puckering the skin between. She didn't understand. How could she?

"That way has a guide. Humans call it a Reaper."

"Humans?" she said and sudden anger sparked in her gaze. "I ask you for honesty and this is what—"

"Look in my eyes, Maggie. Tell me I'm lying."

She stared at him with those blue-green eyes, a hurricane of confusion and rage and hurt . . . and hope swirling inside them. Death had felt like this moment of knowing he would crush that hope.

"I came to take Sam's soul to the afterlife, wherever that might have been for him."

Her lips moved, but nothing came out.

"I was in the room when you told him that you were

sad, but not grieving. That you'd wanted the fairy tale. That he broke your heart."

Her gaze was riveted and now he saw her remembering.

"You were so hurt and so beautiful, but my eyes weren't like yours. What I saw was your essence, not the you I see now. And I couldn't leave until I had more. I wanted to touch you."

Only disbelief showed in her expression. Suspicion tightened her lips, and he knew she thought he was crazy. Just like his ex-wife. Just like she'd thought the real Sam had been in the end.

"You felt me there, Maggie," he said, frustration and anger hardening his voice. He dared her to deny it. "You kept looking at the corner where I stood."

Her eyes rounded, still suspicious but no longer outraged.

"When I moved to stand beside you, I thought if I touched Sam at the moment of reaping, I could hold a piece of him and use it . . . to touch you."

She stepped back and his heart missed a beat.

"So I did. But the doctors shocked his heart at the same time and I was sucked inside with Sam's soul. I was trapped—"

"I felt you," she breathed and her expression cleared.

Confused, he paused, knowing that acceptance hadn't brought that wondrous gleam to her eyes. Somewhere his confession had gone awry.

"I thought I imagined it, but I remember that moment and thinking . . . . Dear God, Sam, are you telling me

86

there's an . . . you're an *angel?*"

Despite his misgivings, hope had risen. Now, it crashed to his feet. "No, Maggie. You don't know how much I wish I could say that it was true. But no, I'm not an angel. I'm a Reaper. Death's courier."

Her face paled and she steadied herself against the wall.

"Sam's memories are fractured and incomplete. His soul is so damaged that I don't know what was done to him. I don't even know *how*. At first, I thought I'd figure that out and move on."

"Move on? You said you were trapped."

"Death would free me."

"Oh my God . . . ."

"I know you must think I'm either crazy or dangerous. Or both. Maybe in the beginning, I was. But not to you—not to the children. Being in this body, being with *you* . . . I was changed from the moment I was trapped, but you have made me something new, Maggie. I *am* what you see when you look into my eyes. I'm no longer a Reaper. I'm no longer human. I don't know what that makes me. Both? Neither? The only thing I know for certain is that I *am* the man you see inside."

Her breath came out in a soft hiss, but she still didn't move. There were so many emotions churning in her eyes that he couldn't begin to guess what they meant. Instead, he tried to close the distance between them, but she held out her hand, stopping him.

"I don't . . . I can't . . . ." She shook her head, tried again. "I . . . I need to think, away from you. Please . . .

go back downstairs. Let me . . . be."

He wanted to refuse—more than anything he wanted to make demands. But survival instincts had come with the skin and he understood that if he pressed, she would leave. She would cast him out of her life forever.

So with a nod, he reluctantly left the room, stopping at the door to say, "*Real* can be a lot of things, Maggie. I'm only just learning that now. But this thing between us . . . it's more real than anything I've ever known. I think it is for you, too."

Feeling like a steel band had clamped around his chest, Sam closed the door behind him.

# CHAPTER THIRTEEN

HE'D HOPED SHE'D come to him that night. He'd stayed awake, praying for the light to go on at the top of the stairs. It never did, and dawn finally stretched its golden fingers through the shutter slats.

When Maggie finally came downstairs, she was quiet and withdrawn. She got the kids ready for school, sharing only a few words with Sam before she left, too, dressed in a pretty blouse, skirt and high heels. She had a showing in Scottsdale, she said in a wooden voice. She'd be back in time to meet Justin at the bus stop.

Each hour of her absence made him antsy, anxious for her return. When the front door finally opened, he looked up hopefully, but it wasn't Maggie. Lexi entered, with a sullen expression and dark circles of blue drawn around her pretty eyes. He didn't know why she put makeup on when she was already so lovely, but those survival instincts he had learned to depend on warned him to keep quiet about it. She shot him a quick glance and started up the stairs.

"You're home early," he said, glancing at the clock in the kitchen. He knew to the minute what time both children came and went.

"Half day," she mumbled.

"Does Justin have one, too?" he asked, worried that no one had met the little boy at the bus stop, then astonished by his own concern. If he'd had any doubts that his integration into humanity was complete, they vanished in that instant.

"He goes to the afterschool program," she said.

He nodded like that meant something and Lexi took another step. "Wait," he said.

The girl paused stiffly.

"I want to talk to you."

She looked down at him from her lofty vantage, anger and confusion vibrating off her in waves he could almost see. Those tentative overtures of trust he'd felt last night had already dissipated.

"Why?" she demanded.

"I need your help," he said honestly. "I don't remember why you hate me. What I did to Maggie. None of it."

She made a disgusted sound. "That's convenient."

"It's the truth. It would make things easier if I knew what I'd done."

"You fucked up," she said, so much rage and hurt in her voice that it cracked.

"Are you supposed to say words like that?"

She shrugged, but a flush stained her cheeks.

"So will you help me?"

Her chin came up, eyes glittering brightly. "What do I get out of it?"

"I won't tell Maggie you're binge watching Sons of

the Arc."

"Anarchy. And she already knows."

"Justin said you weren't supposed to be doing it."

"He's a tattletale."

Sam cocked his head, waiting. "So, will you?"

With a beleaguered sigh, she came down the stairs and flopped on the couch across from him. "What you do want to know?"

"Start at the beginning. Your mother—"

"Egg donor. She was never my mother."

"You hate her more than me," he said, slightly mollified.

She gave him a hard look. "It's a toss-up. But what happened with *her* wasn't your fault. At least, I don't think it was. She's a whack-job. You don't remember any of that?"

He shook his head. "I met her at a funeral. That's the extent of my memory."

"Aunt Celia's funeral," Lexi agreed. "I never knew her, but you used to cry sometimes when you were drinking."

The words sparked a feeling deep inside him. Grief. He chased it into the dark hole where it hid, but lost it before he could put a face and name to it. Evidently, Sam had cared about his sister.

"The egg donor tried to take me and Jus to Mexico one time," Lexi said. "You came home from work and caught her before she took off with us. You never said, but I think she was all drugged up or something. I used to wonder why you ever married her. Now I know."

Interested, he leaned forward. "Why?"

"Me. You knocked her up. You two got married in December. I was born in March."

"Oh." Lexi stared at him like there should have been something else that followed. He tacked on, "Sorry," though he was a bit fuzzy on what he'd apologized for.

"I don't remember her being so bad when I was a kid," she said, like she was a hundred years old now, "but after Justin came, she went off the deep end."

"Did I know she was crazy?"

"You were at work all the time and she never acted that way around you. She always pretended to be the perfect mom when you were home."

It occurred to him that he didn't even know what Sam had done for a living, but it was a sure bet that he'd need to find a different career now—he didn't imagine reaping was listed on any employment sites. A dark voice of humor suggested *undertaker.*

He ignored it and focused on Lexi.

"I didn't notice then how anxious you were?" he asked.

"You remember that?"

The hope in her voice almost made him want to lie. He shook his head. "I just figured . . . ."

"We pretended, too," she said. "Even Jus, and he was only one. When you came home, everything got safe. We didn't want that wrecked, too."

Like a knife, up under his heart. The pain was so strong, so shockingly sharp, that he couldn't speak for a moment.

"I'm sorry things have been so crazy for you," he managed at last.

"*Batshit.*"

He chose to ignore that comment. "And I never caught on? How did the divorce happen, then? Did *she* ask me for it?"

"You really don't remember?" she demanded suspiciously.

Not a damn thing. Was that normal for anyone who didn't want to face their past? Denial, they called it. When she'd sat in the hospital, waiting for him to die, Maggie had said she'd spent months in denial.

"Geez," Lexi said, taking his silence as an answer. "None of it?"

"Nope."

"You filed for divorce after she tried to burn the house down with us in it, just like Maggie said last night. You came home early and stopped her. We stayed at a friend's house for a few days, and when we came home, we were living in an apartment and mom was in the hospital. That's what you told us when we asked. I'm pretty sure it was a mental hospital, but you never said. We were just so happy to be with you."

Her gaze moved over his face, up to the raw scar above his ear. The bandage and stitches were gone and his hair had started to grow around it, but it still looked ugly.

"Who shot you, Dad?" she asked.

It was the first time she'd ever addressed him with the paternal title. Once more, something flipped inside him and lit him with a different kind of panic. He'd been blithely unaware of the hell their mother inflicted, and still this child had once thought him an anchor in a storm. She'd depended on him to keep her safe.

And he'd left her—without a word, according to Maggie.

"I don't know who shot me. The police said I had scratches on my hands, like I'd been in a struggle. I don't remember that either. It's just a big blank from the time we buried your aunt until I woke up in the hospital—except I can remember meeting Maggie."

Lexi had been clutching her backpack in front of her like a shield. Now she let it slip to the ground. "I used to like her," she said. "When you first brought her home."

"What made you stop?"

"You changed after you married her. You got mean. As crazy as *she* was."

"I what?"

Lexi shifted uncomfortably. "I was all excited about having a mom who, you know, didn't want to kill us and all. But then you OD'd on the batshit, too. You were always thinking something was following you. Sometimes it was hound dogs, sometimes—"

"*Hound dogs?*"

She nodded. Could she mean hellhounds? A cold chill went through him. Surely, not?

"And birds. Birds really freaked you out."

"All birds?"

Lexi shot him a weary glance. "Does it matter?"

To him, it did. Ravens were messengers of evil.

Fearing them was a wise choice. But how would Sam know that? Why did he think they were following him? He tried to find a way to ask about demons without sounding *batshit* but couldn't come up with one, so kept quiet.

"Then one night you locked us all in your room upstairs and barricaded the doors."

"Why?"

She raised her brows in an expression that clearly said, *who knows?*

"Nothing ever tried to get in?" he asked.

"Nope. You left after that. Maybe a day or two later. You never even said goodbye. Maggie was pretty torn up."

And Lexi had been devastated. She didn't say it, but she didn't need to. He saw it in her eyes.

"I'm sorry."

She stared at him, but something she read in his expression shut her down. He didn't know what. She stood, jerking her backpack off the floor. "You said that then, too. Are we done now? I have homework."

She didn't give him a chance to respond. Instead, she hurried to the stairs, blue lines around her eyes already smearing as she rubbed away her tears. She'd gone maybe three steps up when something in the air shifted and chilled. It gathered in the corners of the ceiling and seeped down to the floor.

Sam stood and crossed to the base of the staircase just as Lexi paused and glanced around with a frown.

"Lex, come back down," he said carefully, as calmly

95

as he could.

Lexi had confirmed his fears. Before Sam had disappeared, he'd believed hellhounds and ravens were following him. He'd barricaded his family inside, afraid of what else was coming.

This thing in their house now was dead—a spirit— but more than that. Before, he'd feared that Sam had sold his soul, but he'd discarded the idea. Now he considered a different option. Whoever—whatever—this dead thing was, it *felt* of demon.

Had it tried to corrupt Sam's soul and damaged it without successfully laying claim to it?

"Lexi, honey. Come back down."

She gave him a quizzical look. Disconcerted, but not yet afraid.

Beside her, the air thickened like gel, blurring the wall behind it. It seemed to surge from the flat surface, a pulsing disease. Lexi spun to face it just as it erupted a second time, making her stumble back. She tripped over her feet and lost her balance. Sam raced forward, catching her an instant before she plummeted onto the tile landing.

"You okay?" he asked, holding her tight as he searched the room for the thing that reeked of threat. He could feel it like a predator watching them, stalking them. Ghost or demon? He didn't know. Lexi tried to squirm out of his grasp but he held her tight.

"Do you see anything?" he asked in a low, urgent voice. Justin had seen it; maybe she could, too.

Her eyes widened and he saw the wary light enter

them. *Batshit.* That's what her expression said. The phone ringing in the kitchen made her look away. Sam glanced at it, but didn't dare leave Lexi to answer it.

Whatever waited in this house, the Reaper who'd become a part of Sam Sloan knew that running would only make it worse. He needed to show himself—his natural, terrible Reaper self—but how could he do that with Lexi in his arms?

*When you came home, everything got safe.*

She didn't feel safe, now, did she? She thought him crazy like her mother and *real* father had been before. Sam took a deep breath and let it out. If she knew the truth, Lexi would likely see no difference between the dark entity he felt moving around them and the man masquerading as her dad. If he kept the truth hidden, the lurking demon might make the point moot and steal from him this life he shouldn't be living.

Lexi's phone rang, but it was in the backpack on the stairs and before she could move away to answer it, a sound he couldn't identify hissed against the windows. Grit, caught in a gust? No, the rapid, scratching noise had a meatier tone to it.

"What was that?" Lexi asked.

"I don't know. Stay here." For once she didn't argue, and cautiously, he moved to the window and adjusted the slats so he could see out. Birds covered the front yard in a bobbing, jittery blanket. They'd settled in the tree by the front door, on the grass, on the driveway. A big one sailed over them and landed on the porch with black wings stretched high and its beak open.

There was no way this was a good thing.

The ravens from the Beyond—because undoubtedly that's what they were—had humanlike eyes and a queerly malevolent focus. At one time, they'd worked for a specific demon, a vicious one who hated humans and had devoted his existence to destroying them. Lately, the birds had been free agents, working for any number of masters. Who had sent these?

"What time will Justin be getting home?" he asked in a strained voice.

"Like an hour. What's going on?"

Sam had no idea what the black birds wanted. For all he knew, they were here for him. Whatever his next move, though, he didn't have long to make it.

# CHAPTER FOURTEEN

WEARING HER FAVORITE realtor outfit—a coral skirt and matching flowered blouse—Maggie had driven to Scottsdale on autopilot, making turns at her navigator's prompts and pulling up to the property she had listed, so wrapped up in her thoughts that after she parked in the drive, she just sat there.

Yesterday, Sam had rocked her world. Last night, he'd rocked it right off its axis.

He'd told her he was a reaper. *A reaper.* What the hell did she do with that? It was so outlandish that she couldn't even consider believing it.

And yet . . . .

What she'd seen in his eyes had been so raw, so naked and undeniably honest. Not a hint of crazy had lurked around the edges. He absolutely believed what he said . . . which meant he *must* be crazy . . . right?

And yet . . . .

She *had* sensed someone—something—in the corners of the hospital room that day. She'd felt it coming closer. She'd even thought it touched her. An angel . . . that's what she told herself it must be. Or Sam's soul, moving on. She'd found a way to accept both explanations.

If Sam had told her last night that he was an angel, she would have believed him. But a reaper? How could she even begin to wrap her head around that?

She sighed and banged her head against the steering wheel. She didn't have time to think about this now. Her clients would be here soon and if they arrived to find her like this, they'd likely keep driving. With a deep breath, Maggie got out.

The morning air was cool for the end of May in Arizona, but as she stepped from the SUV, it didn't feel fresh. The smell reminded her of . . . yes, that dank odor she'd caught a whiff of in Justin's closet. Strange, oddly disturbing, and completely unfamiliar. Frowning, she moved up the pristine walkway, the hairs on her neck standing on end and a shiver tickling down her spine.

This was an older property with mature landscaping. Two giant Chinese elms spread their branches wide, offering solid shade that blotted out the sun with dense efficiency. Beneath them, it was almost gloomy. She'd asked the property owners to plant flowers around the walk in an effort to brighten it up. Now, neat little rows of vibrant yellow and deep orange blossoms escorted her to the door.

But they didn't alleviate the dismal air hanging so thickly that she felt she might touch it if she tried.

Her code worked in the lockbox hanging from the knob and she stepped into the quiet, locking the door behind her automatically—an old habit she'd developed over the years when she'd lived alone. Setting her purse on the counter in the kitchen, she began her usual prep, opening all the curtains and blinds, turning on lights. The house was empty so there was no clutter to stash or furniture to rearrange. She lit the cinnamon candle on the counter and did a quick tour anyway—just to make sure everything was in place. It all looked perfect until she returned downstairs.

The candle was out and all the curtains were closed tight. She stared at them, knowing that she hadn't imagined opening them a few minutes ago. Nervously, she looked around, methodically checking that both the front and back doors were locked. Digging her mace out of her purse, Maggie moved through the house again, room by room, checking behind doors, looking in closets. Finding nothing but shadows. She had no explanation for the curtains, but already her mind was trying to work out a valid excuse. Maybe the rods were warped and they'd drifted back. It could happen—she'd seen it happen—but never so quickly and on every window. Still, she'd verified that the house was deserted, and since she didn't have any other explanations, she decided to believe the one that made her feel better.

Cautiously, she went back downstairs and opened the curtains again, noting that yes, they slid all too easily on the rods. With bright sun spilling in and the candle lit once more, Maggie pulled out her phone and scrolled through her emails while she waited for her clients, ignoring the weird, menacing feeling that seemed to float in the dust mites. Things had been nuts in her world for the past two weeks, and Sam's declaration had only added to it. She refused to let herself become freaked out by the weighted silence that had closed in.

Today was a half day of school and Lexi should be home by now. Justin went to the after school program and wouldn't be finished until two-thirty. The mundane facts grounded her. She'd have plenty of time to show the house, lock it up and get back before Justin needed to be picked up. She sent Lexi a text, "Home?" and waited for an answer. A few seconds later, "Yes."

Such were the meaningful conversations they held. Sighing, she slipped her phone back into the side pocket of her purse.

Her clients should be here any moment. She gave the curtains a worried glance and went to wait by the front door.

As she approached the foyer, a harsh wind suddenly howled and buffeted against the house, and the front door swung slowly open. Her footsteps faltered as she stared it, while her mind spun through a rapid fire of possible explanations. None stuck. The door had been shut tight and locked. She'd checked it twice.

But now it was open and the gusty wind had gathered up dead leaves and loose grit, spinning them into dervishes. Quickly, she rushed to the door so she could shut it before all that dirt blew in. That's when she noticed the flowers.

The neatly planted rows had been yanked up and tossed across the yard and out into the street. Stunned by the vandalism, she stepped outside, dirt devil forgotten as she surveyed the damage.

She looked up and down the deserted street, feeling

suddenly isolated and afraid. Open curtains, doused candles and exhumed flowers weren't usually the stuff of nightmares, but down to her bones, Maggie felt threatened. The flowers hadn't been in the earth long and they'd come free in compact little sections that looked like corpses in the murky shadows. No culprits were in sight. No fading footsteps to confirm this was all the work of neighborhood pranksters.

An eerie scratching sound spun her around. Her SUV was parked in the driveway. The vehicle wasn't new, but Maggie kept it in mint condition, despite having to haul two kids around. She had to. Usually she was driving her clients, not meeting them. The vehicle was a pretty blue that shimmered in the sun, but while she'd been inside, someone had gouged deep scratches in the hood and doors. Random, intersecting lines that marred every panel and looped around handles and windows. The haphazard scratches seemed profane and threatening. She stared at them in horror until the slamming front door spun her around yet again.

The wind stopped completely in the space of a breath, leaving the air so still it seemed solid. Thick and tight. Shrink wrap to her fear.

One of the elms groaned and a flash of black moved among the branches. Maggie yelped, backing up as it emerged, sailing from the gloom to the rain gutter over the garage.

A broken laugh bubbled up. A bird. Nothing but a bird. But another dark flutter drew her attention back to the yard and held it captive.

Scattered among the mutilated flowers sat dozens of big, black birds. An entire flock from the numbers, all looking at her. She'd never seen so many in one yard. Never knew they grew to be so big. More landed on the roof; the railing of the front porch. The one perched on the gutter over the garage cocked its head and stared at her with shiny, round eyes. It opened its beak, flashing a black maw as it squawked angrily.

Maggie took another step back, so close to a meltdown that she could barely move. There were so many and they kept coming, as if some birdy dinner bell had been rung. They fluttered and ruffled, cawed and pecked, irritating one another, squawking vehemently.

She glanced over her shoulder. The neighbor's yard looked pristine. Not even a dove perched in the trees. Same thing on the other side and across the street.

*We can hurt you,* a voice whispered in her head. *Peck, peck, peck at your eyes.*

Black wings spread wide and the big one—Jesus she'd never seen a bird so big—soared down from the gutter, skimming the air with those oily feathers, long spindly feet hanging, claws curled. It came right at her. Maggie shrieked, ducked and covered her head. Its talons grazed the flesh of her forearm, leaving burning welts behind. Suddenly all of the birds took to the air, dive bombing, backing her down the walk. They dragged their claws through her hair, snagged her blouse and scratched the arms she held over her head to protect her face.

She screamed and flailed, trying to run, but she couldn't see where she was going. She stumbled over the walk, catching the toe of her shoe in one of the holes left from the uprooted flowers. She fell head- first into the grass, skinning her knees and tearing her skirt. The birds swooped down on her instantly, claws and beaks everywhere. She scrambled to her feet, kicking off her heels as she dashed to her SUV, but her purse was inside on the counter, and the SUV would be locked because she always locked it, just in case.

Like wasps, the ravens swarmed around her and all she could do was fight them off as she bolted back to the house, convinced the door would be locked against her, suspicious when it wasn't. She slammed it hard when they tried to follow her in. One succeeded. The fat one that had seemed to speak.

Good God, she'd lost her mind.

She was panting, gasping and crying all at once. Her entire body shook with reaction. She leaned against the door, refusing to give into the insane fear that made her want to keep screaming.

"You're safe, you're safe," she whispered, as if that would convince her it was true. "Just one bird. It can't hurt you."

But it could, and they both knew it. The creature opened its beak in a macabre chuckle.

"*Ha!*" she shouted and stomped her foot at it.

The bird scuttled back a few steps but looked amused by her efforts to scare it. Suddenly, Maggie's fear turned to rage. Whatever madness this was, she'd had enough. She forced herself forward, charging the stupid bird like she wasn't terrified. It took flight, circling the vast living room. It perched on the chandelier that dangled in the foyer.

*They're mine. You can't have them.*

She didn't know what that meant, but was pretty sure it had something to do with her sanity.

Maggie kept her eyes on the raven as she backed into the kitchen, bare feet damp and slippery on the tile. Without looking away from the vile raven—crow— whatever it was, she snatched her purse off the counter, holding it against her chest as she dug out her phone. Her hand shook so hard she had to enter her password twice. Blood welled up in the scratches on her arms and they stung like they'd been filled with acid. Her trembling finger hovered over the keypad. She wanted to dial nine-one-one, but what would she say to the emergency operator? Someone had closed her curtains, dug up her flowers and sent a flock of black birds to scare her? She'd probably end up arrested or committed. Maybe they'd give her the padded room next to Janet's.

She wanted to breakdown and cry. She wanted to call Sam and tell him to come get her. He wouldn't laugh at her, wouldn't make her feel like she'd lost her mind. She knew that in a deep place that only spoke truth. But he didn't even have a car anymore—at least not that he remembered—and she still felt leery about depending on him. It was too soon for that.

Besides, there was the whole *Reaper Thing.*

Yet her fingers moved, dialing the house phone since Sam didn't have a cell anymore. It rang relentlessly until the machine picked up. Where was he? Fear curdled in her stomach. Had he vanished again just like last time? She tapped *End* and tried Lexi's phone. It rang and rang without answer, too.

*Fuck.*

The vulgar word sounded strong in her head and it stiffened her spine. Still watching the raven on the chandelier, she moved to the window and aimed her key fob. The SUV's lights flashed and the faint *thunk* of the locks releasing reached her ears. The birds on the lawn all turned their heads in unison, daring her to make a break. Her arms had a hundred scratches on them, her shirt had been torn, and her skirt was ripped up the seam in the back from when she'd fallen. The thought of going back out there terrified her.

*Don't you know who we are, Miss Fancy Pants?*

Cold sweat covered her body. Janet had called her that the day she'd warned Maggie that the family she loved wouldn't belong to her for long.

She shot a look at the bird. It stared back with those round eyes, so intent that she wanted to scream again. In her mind, she plotted her escape route. She still didn't know who had ripped out the flowers—the birds couldn't have done that, right?—but whoever had could be in the house right now. Which would be worse? Claws and beaks... *peck, peck, peck at your eyes . . .*

or whoever waited, hidden somewhere inside?

She didn't know, but she couldn't stay here.

With a deep breath, she moved to the hall where the laundry room opened into the garage. The bird shifted so it could watch her progress. It realized her destination too late. The big wings spread and the raven dove just as she stepped into the laundry room and shut the door. She heard the thud of its body as it bounced off the panels and onto the tile. Instantly, the beak poked under the gap at the floor.

She clapped her hand over her mouth and fumbled for the knob of the door behind her. The garage smelled of oil and paint. She stood on the cold concrete barefoot, wrecked and shaking all over. Purse clutched to her side, car keys firmly in hand, she pushed the button on the wall and started to run, braced for the attack. A scream was lodged somewhere in her throat; she couldn't get it out and she couldn't breathe around it.

Bending to slip under the lifting door, Maggie came out in sunshine, quiet . . . and face-to-face with her stunned clients.

# CHAPTER FIFTEEN

SAM NEEDN'T HAVE worried about delaying his next move. The thing that stalked them had little patience. The smear that appeared against the wall took shape, then color. Horrified, he and Lexi watched as it solidified into human form. Justin had always referred to it as *she*. Now, he knew why.

Hazy around the edges, but undeniably female, the thing had long matted hair and wore tattered, bloody clothes. One side of its head had caved in, leaving gore and blood to streak what was left of its face and trail in rivulets down its throat. The blouse it had on might once have been blue, but dirt and blood had seeped into the fibers making it a rusted gray. Jeans still covered its hips and legs, but only one shoe was on its feet. Every exposed inch of skin had wounds and withering flesh. Freshly dead, just as he'd suspected when he'd first caught its scent in Justin's closet.

"Dad," Lexis said fearfully. "Do you see it?"

"I see it," he answered grimly.

A spirit like any other he'd ferried to the other side, yet this one hadn't made its journey and the *why* rode its shoulders like a cape. The demon was small and black, a slithering entity that had sunk deep talons into the spirit it held.

He didn't understand that. If this female had bargained with her soul, the demon should have taken her back to its lair and feasted in the way demons were wont to do. Why was it here? What did it wait for?

"Dad," Lexi said again, turning her face into his chest as his arms came around. "Is that Mom?"

He would never know if it was the whimpered question . . . his daughter's fear . . . or perhaps simply the moment of reckoning that did it, but suddenly the floodgates in his head opened up and all the memory that had hidden behind the blank slate of his brain burst forth. Images slammed against his mind, leaving swift impressions, out of order, nonsensical . . . right up until the point when it all came together.

Janet—yes, it was her. It had always been her. She'd been released from the facility that had cared for her last year. He hadn't known. By then he was married to Maggie. Janet had shown up at work, looking normal, sane . . . wanting to see the children.

He knew the kids would never heal until they had some closure with her. He'd hoped that somehow the treatment she'd undergone had cured her. But she'd grown angry when he'd insisted she see them under supervision and left in a fury. For a few days, he'd hoped . . . God how he'd hoped.

He hadn't known that she'd found more than mental help in the hospital. She'd found a way to talk to the demons that had been in her head. She'd made a deal—a two-for-one bargain with the demon who lived off her soul now. She'd infected Sam with its corruption and it had begun to eat away his mind, making him erratic, psychotic, paranoid—all of the symptoms Maggie and the kids remembered. He'd run away to escape and to protect them, just as the Reaper had suspected all along.

But he'd made a mistake. He'd come back and Janet had found him.

Sam staggered, pulling Lexi back with him as the final moments of his old life washed over him. Janet had lain in wait at his apartment, confronted him with a gun and shot him when he still refused to join her in the glory of the dark side. She'd planned the murder to the moment, knowing that his corrupted soul would be unable to resist the demon once the body was dead.

But she'd left him to die instead of killing him outright . . . and she hadn't counted on a certain Reaper who'd stepped in and changed the game.

His last memory before the hospital was of watching her get in his car and drive away while his blood drained onto the asphalt.

So how and when had she died? How had they come to this point?

He didn't have time to find out. He needed to protect Lexi, get her out of this toxic place before the thing that Janet had become decided to use his daughter as a pawn. He pushed Lexi behind him, and stepped to the door just as it opened and Maggie limped in, dressed in an oversized t-shirt and stretchy pants. Angry scratches covered her arms and terror filled her eyes.

111

And Justin entered right behind her.

# CHAPTER SIXTEEN

THERE WERE TOO many things for Maggie to take in all at once. She saw Sam first, standing at the edge of the foyer, his face pale, his eyes wide with . . . fear? Is that what she saw? Lexi was right behind him, clinging to his arm. She was definitely afraid, but of what? From outside, an engine revved as a car came around the corner and stopped in front of her house. She glanced back, saw Detectives Hartman and Bulldog get out, drawn expressions on their faces.

"Maggie," Sam said. "Take Justin and go outside."

"What's going—"

"Now, Maggie."

"It's her," Justin cried.

Maggie looked down at Justin and followed the line of his gaze to a point on the stairs. And from there, all rational thought vanished.

An apparition stood halfway down. It was a woman dressed in ragged clothing, missing a shoe. She had long, straggly hair and a bloody face that had been bashed in on one side.

It took only a moment to realize that the apparition was Janet.

She was filthy and stank of the same odor Maggie had smelled at the Scottsdale property.

Sam was inching his way to the door, Lexi still cowering behind him. When he drew even with Maggie, he said, "Get the kids out of here."

And finally, Maggie toppled over the edge into belief. He'd been telling the truth all along.

"You come with us, Sam," she said.

Janet began to descend the stairs in an awkward gait that was neither walking nor floating. Each step seemed to require focus and skill. Maggie could see the frustration in Janet's eyes as she navigated the uneven stairway and her stomach rolled as she watched the unnatural movements. Seeing the ghost of Sam's ex-wife made his claim of being a Reaper somehow tangible. Logical. *Truth.* She didn't have time to analyze why. She could only accept what her gut told her.

"Sam . . . ."

"She's here for me, Maggie. She's why I left."

"You remember?"

He nodded, his eyes filled with agony. "There's only one way to fight her," he said softly.

The thing gave up on the stairs and moved to the wall, climbing it like a spider, its head twisted round so it could watch Sam as it circumvented the foyer, moving up and around in order to reach him.

It would be on them in seconds. Sam pulled Lexi out from behind him and shoved her at Maggie.

"Get out."

"But what are you going to do?" she cried.

"She came for me," he repeated and the look he gave her was filled with remorse. "The only way to keep her from you is to take her out."

Take her out? Maggie frowned, working the pieces of that statement into sense. Suddenly she understood. *Reap her.* That's what he meant.

It took only a second for Maggie to see what he planned. He'd said death would free him—free the reaper he'd been before he'd been trapped inside of her husband's body. Any doubt she'd held—even after the birds, even after cleaning her wounds in the restroom at Target where she'd stopped for clothes so as not to alarm Justin when she picked him up—vanished in an instant.

Sam strode to the kitchen, giving one last command over his shoulder. "Out, Maggie. I don't want you or the kids to see this."

The children. Yes, she had to protect them. But how could she let Sam do this?

She didn't know what she felt for him . . . lust . . . hate . . . anger . . . love? Sam was a labyrinth she'd been navigating since the day she'd spilled her coffee on his shoes. This new Sam was no less complex. Yet there was a core of goodness in him—there always had been. And through the iterations, through the good and bad, the sane and crazy, that core had never changed. What he was now and what he'd been before . . . the two shared more than skin. Death and rebirth hadn't changed that. And the truth was, she loved him.

It didn't make sense, and at the same time, it made perfect sense.

Whatever he'd been, whatever he'd become . . . she loved who he was now.

"Sam," she cried as the creature crawled overhead, following him like a nightmare dog. She pulled the kids backwards, out the open door, sobbing, unable to think beyond the tragedy that was unfolding right before her eyes. The children were hysterical, crying for their father.

"What's he doing?" Lexi demanded at the same time Justin cried, "What's he going to do—"

"Mrs. Sloan?" a voice interrupted sharply.

She and the kids spun to see the detectives right behind them. Hartman took one look at their faces and pulled his gun.

"No," she cried, but he and Bulldog had already charged through the door. "Stay here," she told Lexi and Justin as she followed.

What happened next, she'd never understand, yet some part of her brain catalogued the sequence and documented what she saw. The two detectives entered, weapons drawn and ready. Sam was in the kitchen, a butcher knife in his hand. He meant to kill himself with that blade and Maggie screamed at the horror and wrongness of it. The thing that had once been Janet was pinned to the wall, watching him with greedy eyes, unaware of the end that raced toward them all. Maggie saw something shifting around Janet's shoulders like a black shawl. She didn't know what it was.

"Hands in the air, Sloan. Drop the knife," Bulldog shouted, obviously mistaking Sam as a threat to Maggie and the kids.

He didn't see the creature on the wall. Maggie knew because he didn't even glance at it. Hartman, though, stared with wide, aghast eyes.

In a moment that was frozen for uncountable heartbeats, Sam shifted his gaze to Maggie. "I love you," he said. "I finally know what that means."

The Janet-thing shrieked with rage and jumped at Sam. Maggie saw decision flash through his eyes. In an instant, he'd turned to the cops and charged with the knife held out in front of him, forcing their hand.

Hartman shouted, "No," just as Bulldog pulled the trigger.

Sam's body slammed back into the island, knife falling from his hand. His eyes began to glaze and he turned to Maggie once more as she tried to rush forward. Hartman caught her around the waist and held her back.

Maggie sensed something rise from Sam's body like a cool mist on a dusky night. The thing that was Janet shrieked again, this time in terror. It turned in a scuttling circle and tried to get away, but the misty cloak found her, covered her . . . *reaped her.*

"What the fuck," Hartman said as Bulldog went down on his knees in front of Sam's body, pulling out a phone and calling for emergency medical support as he tried to staunch the blood.

The black cloak around Janet's shoulders separated and vanished like smoke in the wind. A moment later, the mist had dissipated, taking Janet and the stench of death with it.

# CHAPTER SEVENTEEN

THE REAPER TUCKED himself in shadow at the back of the room, weighed down by emotions no Reaper had ever felt before. Sam Sloan lay on the bed, his skin the color of paste. He should be dead, but machines kept his body breathing. The Reaper knew Maggie was to blame for that. She'd insisted.

A doctor came in—the second one in the past hour. Maggie had sat beside the hospital bed since they'd wheeled Sam out of surgery, not moving even when the two detectives had come to see her.

Hartman had witnessed what had happened at the house, though he didn't speak of it. The Reaper knew he never would. The other detective had no clue, but he was riddled with guilt once Maggie explained that Sam had acted in self defense, believing his family was in danger. The wound to his head, she'd told them, had made him act irrationally.

The two had come to tell them that they'd found Janet Sloan's body in a ravine near Camelback Mountain. The coroner had verified that the time of death had been during the long days when Sam had been recovering from the gunshot wound, in the hospital under round-the-clock surveillance, an iron-clad alibi. They'd determined that Janet had shot herself, staging the suicide so that her body would plummet to the ravine in death. She'd probably thought it would disguise the self-inflicted nature of her wounds.

Maggie had calmly thanked them for seeing the case through and wished them a good day. They'd left with questions—especially Hartman—but after struggling to form them without sounding *batshit* himself, Hartman and his partner had left.

"Mrs. Sloan," the doctor said now. "I know this is difficult. Sam's recovery before was a miracle, but this time . . . ." He shook his head. "There's no brain activity. Before he was breathing on his own and—"

"No," she said. "I won't do it. He'll come back to me. I know he will."

The Reaper smiled and the heart he shouldn't have swelled at her stubbornness. The doctor left and Maggie turned her gaze to his corner. He remembered the first time he saw those fascinating eyes. He'd been entranced from the start.

"I don't know if you're there," she said. "But I'm not going to leave until they drag me out."

He stepped forward and her gaze snapped to him, though he knew she couldn't actually see him. The first time, she'd been disquieted by his presence. Now, he sensed hope.

"I'm sorry I didn't listen when you tried to tell me the truth. I didn't know . . . I didn't understand. But I saw what you did for us, Sam. You gave yourself to keep us safe. Now come back to me. I love you. Please come back to me."

He took another step, afraid to believe what he heard. It might be guilt, grief, any number of the vast array of human emotions which he now understood. He'd been wrong to wedge his way into her life before. She deserved a human mate who would give her the human life she'd always dreamed of, not him. Never him.

"I'm not looking for the fairy tale anymore, Sam. I'm only looking for you. I don't care what you are, what you were . . . I only care what you're going to be. That's mine. Until death do us part."

Had he heard that right? Did she truly mean it?

The monitor beside his bed bleeped. Maggie sniffed and looked up, dark brows pulled. Anxiously, her gaze shifted from the monitor to the prone man.

"It's time, Sam. Please. Come back to me."

The machine made another strident sound and a nurse rushed in with two doctors right behind them.

The Reaper moved to the bed. Maggie's gaze jerked to the corner and tracked back until it rested on him once again. He didn't know how she knew.

"I feel you," she breathed.

"Mrs. Sloan . . . Maggie," the doctor said. "It's time."

Maggie shook her head. "No," she said. "Save him."

"But—"

"Please."

"But—"

"Save him."

The doctor gave her a hard look, but finally nodded and Maggie moved to the end of the bed where she could see without being in the way.

*Hurry, Sam. Hurry.*

Her lips moved and the Reaper felt the words even though she never spoke.

She caught her breath when he touched her and her pulse beat an erratic tempo at the base of her throat. Her eyes rounded, the beautiful blues and greens mixing and changing as she turned her face up to him.

One of the nurses pulled the blanket off, unveiling Sam's muscular body. The gown came down to bunch at his waist as another nurse pushed a cart in the room. Maggie turned to watch them, hope in her eyes.

The Reaper moved over Samuel Sloan, seeping beneath his skin to the soul that had endured so much. It was still there . . . weak, but no longer tainted with corruption. He'd vanquished the demon when he'd taken Janet to the other side.

Somewhere in the room a doctor said, "Clear," and pressed paddles to Sam's chest. The Reaper braced himself for the searing pain that sliced through to the core of him, impaling them both. He welcomed the agony.

The doctor said, "Clear," once more. A second volt jolt went through Sam, through the Reaper, down to a place where the Reaper waited. He didn't fight it this time and in an instant, it was done.

Joy filled him. He felt Maggie touch his leg as she circled the bed and came up to his side.

"I don't know what you hoped for, Maggie," the

doctor said gently. "But . . . ."

"Could you unplug the machines now?" she asked.

"What?"

"He doesn't need them anymore."

"Before we do that, we need to know . . . Sam was a healthy man. His organs could go to—"

"Please unplug the machines. My husband is going to need his organs."

The Reaper fought his way to the surface, letting the human body mold to him once more. It felt like coming home, a home he vowed to never leave again.

The bright lights burned his eyes when they opened. The sharp gasp from the doctors rang in his ears.

And the first word from his lips was, "Maggie."

—The End—

KEEP READING FOR A PREVIEW OF

# THE FIVE DEATHS
# OF ROXANNE LOVE

# THE FIVE DEATHS
## OF ROXANNE LOVE

## ERIN QUINN

## CHAPTER ONE

THE REAPER ENTERED the room as Santo Castillo spun the cylinder of the revolver, took a deep swallow of Wild Turkey, then put the muzzle in his mouth. He pulled the trigger without hesitation. The hollow click that followed seemed to mock the shadowed silence.

Santo choked back a sob, dropped the gun on the low coffee table in front of him, and reached for his glass again. For a long moment he just sat there, shoulders hunched, silent, dry sobs wracking his body. A tall man, with broad shoulders and a heavy, muscular frame, he looked odd crying his dry tears. The reaper moved closer, perplexed by the duplicity of human emotion. The man wanted to die. He begged for death, yearned for it. And yet he fought it even now, when it was too late.

The reaper paused just behind him and blew a soft breath in his ear. Santo stiffened, lifted his head, and looked around uneasily.

*Yes. I've come for you.*

A shudder went through the human and he took another hasty drink, wincing as the burn of the alcohol slid down his throat.

A light hung just above the couch and coffee table where Santo wallowed in his misery. The reaper gave it a gentle nudge, making it sway back and forth, producing cadaverous shadows that slithered across the walls. The chain squeaked ever so slightly in a macabre overture to what would come. Santo's gaze darted warily around the room. His fear seasoned the air and the reaper breathed it in. Fear always honeyed the reaping.

He moved closer, trailing his fingers over Santo's broad shoulders, admiring the hard strength of him. Yes, he would be perfect.

*Perfect,* he whispered.

Santo jumped and spun in his seat, staring right through the reaper, seeing nothing but the queer bogeymen of his imagination. His anxious eyes grew hot with panic as he turned back around. The small hairs on his nape stood on end. Santo reached for his gun and fumbled, sending it in a tailspin across the table, knocking over a framed snapshot he'd propped in front of him—a silent witness to his madness. The gun skated off the smooth surface and hit the carpeted floor with a dull thud.

While Santo ducked down to retrieve it, the reaper righted the photo.

Visibly shaken, his pulse a staccato beat at his throat, Santo closed his eyes and rubbed the scruff of his beard. He mumbled something the reaper couldn't hear, but then again, he didn't need to hear it. They all prayed at this point.

After several deep breaths, Santo opened his eyes again and focused on the framed picture, once more positioned on the table. The image of a jubilant Santo with dark, sparkling eyes and a wide, dimpled smile looked back from the photograph. Wrapped around him from behind was a female with the same brown skin and velvety gaze. She laughed at the camera.

The reaper remembered her. He'd been the one to take her when her time had come. She and her baby had tasted of sweetness and light, and as he'd passed them through to their next destination, he'd been strangely moved by a sense of loss.

He frowned with distaste at the memory. He blamed another woman for the unwanted emotion. Roxanne Love. Before her, he'd never cared for the souls he'd reaped. Only that they'd abounded.

He watched Santo as the human scowled at the righted photograph. The reaper could see the memory of the last few moments replaying in Santo's mind, in his expression. The spinning gun careening toward the snapshot, the frame teetering, toppling over with a flat, cracking sound that had left a splinter in the glass at the bottom right corner. Santo's eyes shifted back and forth as he recounted each cause and effect in an attempt to rationalize how the frame could have come to be propped in front of him now, as if none of that had happened.

Santo shook his head in silent denial. Looking like the cop he'd been for the last twelve years, he narrowed his dark eyes and searched the room.

*You know who I am. You invited me here.*

The human's fear simmered to an erotic terror. He gave the gun in his hand a desperate look, took another drink, and shoved the muzzle in his mouth. The cruel click of the pulled trigger taunted him, as impotent as the dry tears.

He savored Santo's anguish. Few humans really desired death when they courted it in this manner. This one did, yet Santo felt he deserved the torture of the game he played. He owned half a dozen guns that would have done the job quicker, but he endured the punishment of each deadly click. The torment of forcing himself to do it again and again.

The reaper knew Santo would keep pulling that trigger, until the job was done. At 12:10 a.m., a clean shot would blow away the back of his skull and kill him instantly.

Or should.

For Santo Castillo, death would come, but not from a bullet. His beautiful face would remain intact, his gray matter safely stored in his cranium. The reaper had never taken a soul from a human that still lived, but he didn't hesitate to do it now. He needed a body for a day, maybe less. Just long enough to find the woman who'd escaped him. The woman whose soul he'd touched, held, and lost. Just long enough to reap her and return to the Beyond.

In less than twenty-four hours Roxanne Love would die once again. Only this time he'd be there, in flesh and spirit, to make sure she *stayed* dead.

4

As Santo put the gun in his mouth once more, the reaper sat down on the table in front of him and let himself be *seen*. For a single, glorious moment, Santo's terror swaddled them both, then the reaper took over and put an end to the human's misery.

# CHAPTER TWO

FIFTY-EIGHT MINUTES before she died, Roxanne Love noticed three things. The stain on the ceiling, her brother's short fuse, and the tall stranger who quietly entered and sat in the back.

The stain had caught her eye earlier, and after that, she couldn't stop looking at it. A stain meant a leak and that meant a bill. Bad news all around. But worse than that, the black splotch crouching in the far corner like a fat spider gave her a bad case of the creeps, though she couldn't say just why. The crazy feeling stalked her as she served drinks to the two customers sitting at the bar of the pub she co-owned with her brothers and sister. She couldn't shake it.

Then the man came through the front door.

Six and half feet, sporting the kind of muscle that took work to build, he strode in like he was on a mission. He wore a black T-shirt beneath a weathered leather jacket that looked like it might have been brown at one time but had faded to a distressed shade of beige. Jeans hugged his long legs and a whole lot of masculine mojo followed him like fanfare.

He took a seat in the corner, seeming to pull all the shadows in around him. The observation was so strange that she almost laughed. Almost.

"What can I get for you?" she asked, setting a cocktail napkin in front of him.

"Wild Turkey," he ordered in a smoky voice that teased her a step closer.

He was ridiculously attractive with all that dark brooding attitude and he-man brawn. In contrast, he had the longest eyelashes she'd ever seen. Thick and black, they framed smoldering eyes the color of midnight.

"Please," he tacked on when she stood there staring.

Embarrassed, she asked, "Straight up or on the rocks?"

"In a glass," he answered with a bewildered frown.

She might have laughed if he hadn't seemed so serious.

"That's generally where we pour them," she said. "The floor is just too messy."

His startled expression became a slow grin that made her blush to her roots. He was *that* good looking. At the same time, a niggling sense of disquiet wormed its way into her addled brain.

"I'll be right back with your drink," she mumbled.

As she turned away, the stain caught her eye again and her unease tipped into foreboding. The power of the feeling on the heels of her embarrassment gave it a disproportionate weight that made it all the more disturbing. What the hell was wrong with her tonight?

She served the man's drink quickly, avoiding his eyes and returning to the safety of the bar like an awkward teenager with a really bad crush.

A minute later her twin brother pushed through the swinging door from the kitchen. "86 the meatloaf," Reece said, eyeing the deserted bar and tables. "We should just close up for the night."

"Ryan says not before midnight." Ryan was their older brother and the boss.

"Ryan says," Reece mocked.

He caught sight of the man sitting in the corner and paled.

"Who's that?" he demanded, turning his back as he filled his cup with ice and soda.

"A customer?" she answered.

He scowled at her. "I don't think so. He looks like a cop."

Surprised, Roxanne gave the man in question a glance. He didn't look like a cop to her, but he had this dark, sexy as sin, *if George Clooney were Latino* thing going on that leant him a mysterious, dangerous air. He'd walked in like a he had a purpose, though. Now he sat cloaked in all that shadow and manliness. It was unnerving. *He* was unnerving. And he'd been watching her since he'd come in.

She knew, because she'd been watching him back.

"What does it matter if he's a cop?" she asked Reece, trying not to look at the man again. "We're not breaking the law. We're serving food and drinks, just like it says we do on the front door. I've been checking IDs. Don't worry about him."

"I'm not worried," Reece snapped.

"Then why are you biting my head off?" She

grabbed his sleeve when he would have turned away. "Seriously. What's up? What's the matter?"

Her brother glanced at the man again before he searched Roxanne's face as if seeking understanding. But she didn't get what he wanted her to understand. In all honesty, it had been a long time since she'd been on the same page with her twin. Not since the *accident*.

"Nothing's going on," Reece said. "I just want to get the fuck out of here."

With that, he filled his cup and went back to the kitchen. A few seconds later, she heard him slamming things around and cursing loud enough that Jim and Sal, regulars who could be found at their bar most any night, could hear him. The two men exchanged glances but said nothing. She felt bad for Manny, their dishwasher, who had to be stuck in the kitchen with Reece for the rest of the night.

She thought about following her brother and forcing him to talk to her, but what was the point? He'd either take his bad mood out on her or whine about having to work on Friday night and she'd heard it all before. Love's had been opened by their grandparents back in the days when Mill Avenue had a producing flour mill and Tempe, Arizona had been a sleepy town. When their father had died, it became theirs. It was a piece of their heritage that they all held onto, even though lately it felt like more labor than love.

With a frustrated sigh, she went back to work, but business was slow and her two customers had full drinks. She wiped the bar, forcing herself *not* to look at the man in the corner or the stain on the ceiling.

But she couldn't help it. Every few minutes she glanced up, eyeing the splotch balefully. Unable to shake the feeling that it was some kind of omen.

She couldn't stop peeping at the stranger in the back either. He sat alone, nursing his Wild Turkey, pretending to mind his own business. But he was still watching her. She could feel it.

If he was a cop, why was he watching *her*?

And what did his presence have to do with Reece being strung so tight? The last time her brother had been such an ass-hat, bad things had happened. Things she didn't even like to remember. The thought of living through them again made her bones ache.

At last, she tossed her towel beneath the bar and decided to quit dancing around and just find out who he was.

"How you doing over here?" she asked, approaching with an easy smile that felt utterly fake.

"I'm fine, thank you for asking," he answered.

His eyes held a bemused gleam as they made a lazy sweep of her hair and face. She caught herself smoothing her ponytail and tried not to look completely disconcerted by him. But it was harder than it should have been. She couldn't stop staring into his bedroom-deep eyes with those long, lush lashes. On any other man, they would have seemed feminine, but the angles of this one's face were too sharp and masculine for that. A couple of scars nicked and wended over his black brow and straight nose, roughing up his features in a way that made his face all

10

the more compelling.

"I haven't seen you in here before," she said, pleased at how natural her voice sounded. It had just the right balance of warmth and inquisitiveness and none of the jittery nerves rioting inside her.

"It's my first visit."

She had the oddest sense that the innocuous statement held a double meaning she wasn't sharp enough to catch.

"Well, welcome to Love's. I'm Roxanne."

"I know. Roxanne Love."

He spoke her name in that husky tone, only now it held a note of satisfaction. As if finding her, recognizing her, had been a great feat that he'd accomplished against all odds.

Her smile faltered and she took a step back. The instinct was ingrained. It had been years since the media or the obsessed fanatics who'd stalked her in the past had caught her unawares, but she never fully let down her guard.

He smiled again. It seemed he couldn't help himself, and a dimple flashed from his cheek. "I've made you nervous."

"No," she lied, "but you have me at a disadvantage. I don't think we've met."

"Not formally."

Not at all. No way she would have forgotten him.

"I'm Detective Santo Castillo," he said and Roxanne released her breath on a soft whoosh.

Okay, so not a stalker. That was good news. But

Reece guessing he was a cop and then freaking out about it…not so great. Not when it made her think her brother must be guilty of something.

The detective leaned across the table and handed her his badge.

Wary, Roxanne studied the medal and verified that the picture matched the man before giving it back. But a bad feeling settled around her. Just like the damn stain, it began to spread. She glanced up again before she could stop herself. As if to confirm a relationship, it had grown bigger and somehow more threatening.

She swallowed and forced her attention back to Santo Castillo. His glass was almost empty. "Drinking on the job, Detective?" she asked, nodding at it.

"Off the clock."

"But not off duty?"

"What cop is ever off duty?"

She supposed he had a valid point, but she was getting too many mixed signals from him to know what to trust.

"So what brings you and your badge to Love's tonight?"

"Good food, fine brew, and great friends," he said, quoting the motto printed on the front window.

"So you're not looking for anyone?"

"Like?"

"I don't know. Outlaws."

"And if I am?" he asked.

She shrugged, glancing at the nearly deserted bar. "Good luck with that?"

A taut pause followed while he snared her gaze and held it prisoner.

"You seem a bit skittish, Roxanne."

She felt a bit skittish. Excited. Like she'd just raced down a long staircase and found that the last step dropped into nowhere.

She balanced on the edge, hyperaware of him. His size. His intensity. His *presence*. She didn't know if she wanted to bolt or move closer. He caught his bottom lip with his teeth and worried it for a moment, while his gaze delivered a message so *male* that she felt an instinctive, uncontrollable response.

He said very softly, "You have beautiful eyes. I didn't expect that."

"What?"

"It's the gold in the gray, I think. It's startling."

She didn't know what to say, so she stood there, speechless, mouth opened in surprise. She'd been told her eyes were pretty before—who hadn't?—but coming from him, it seemed to take a deeper meaning. She felt another hot blush creep up her throat.

"What do you mean, you didn't *expect* it?"

"I've been watching you."

"Yeah, I noticed that. Why?"

The question hung between them, filled with a weight she didn't quite fathom. He seemed to be sifting through his thoughts, examining and discarding responses. At last he said simply, "I find you intriguing."

"That sounds a little creepy considering you've never even met me before," she said.

He laughed, and the sound sent a trill down her spine. She didn't know if he was flirting with her or toying with her. Maybe it didn't matter. She was ill equipped to handle either one.

"You and your brother seem to be having a disagreement tonight," he said, switching the subject so unexpectedly that she had to scramble to keep up.

"I can't see how that's any of your business," she answered.

"Can't you? Why don't you have a seat? Let's talk about my business."

The eyes sparkled wickedly and the disquiet burrowing in the pit of her stomach spread its wings and became full-fledged anxiety. He'd been playing her, keeping her off balance so he could blindside her with his questions. Questions about Reece if she'd read the scenario correctly.

*Reece? What did you do?*

She needed to get back to the kitchen and find out what the hell was going on before the detective mind-melded her with another of those soul-searching looks and she said something stupid. *Stupider,* she corrected.

Roxanne pinned another fake smile in place and said, "Of course, Detective—"

"Santo. You can call me Santo."

*Oh, I think not.*

"Let me just check on things in the kitchen first," she said carefully. "We're about to close up for the night."

He glanced at his watch as if to confirm it and nodded. "By all means. Put your affairs in order."

A really weird way of saying *do what you need to do* that pinged her inner alarms. She wanted to ask what he meant by that, but she glanced up again and all other thoughts vanished as she sucked in a stunned breath.

In the time she'd been talking to him, the stain had spread to the edges of the ceiling. She could see it moving like a wave rushing the shore. The idea that it was alive and with purpose took root in some sequestered part of her psyche and began to grow. She imagined she could even smell it. Dank and sulfurous.

The detective pushed away from the table, staring up at it with sudden anger that was almost as confounding as the speed with which the stain had spread.

As if from a distance, she heard her two regulars, Jim and Sal, talking. Jim muttered, "You smell that? Toilets backed up, you think?"

"Must be," Sal agreed.

She jerked her gaze away and stared at the two men in shock. "Look," she said, her voice squeaking. She jabbed a finger at the ceiling.

They did, both of them coming to their feet as they stared at the seeping blackness overhead. "What the fuck *is* that?" Sal demanded.

"I don't know. It was just a spot earlier, but now—"

A loud buzzing spun them all around to face the front door and windows. The noise seemed to come from just outside. Droning and harsh, it grew in volume and intensity as they watched with mouths open and eyes wide.

Everyone except the detective.

He knew what was coming, knew what made that hideous, atonal sound. She could see it on his face. He scanned from the ceiling to the windows and back, eyes hard, brows pulled.

"What?" she breathed. "What is—"

The first of the bugs hit the window with a squelching pop, and Roxanne screamed, jumping back. Greenish-brown goo splattered out from the point of impact, but she barely had a moment to register it before more slammed into the glass. Hundreds of them peppered it like bullets, leaving behind a nauseating smear of guts and gore. Each impact sent her back another jerky step until she bumped into the bar.

"Why are they doing that?" she demanded to keep from screaming again. She wanted to cover her eyes and ears, but fear of *not* seeing kept her from doing either one.

"Fuck," Sal yelled. "Look at the ceiling."

She tore her gaze away only to see that the stain above had thickened into a slick black ooze. It looked like an upside-down oil spill on a choppy sea. Soon it would reach the bar and the kitchen. And the stench . . . Damp and foul. Rotten eggs in a steamy soup.

The blackness began to drip, and Roxanne fought down another scream.

"Reece! Reece, get out here!" she shouted instead, just as a loud crash came from the kitchen.

*"Reece!"*

Santo turned, his gaze unerringly finding hers. The look he gave her spoke volumes, but she couldn't understand what it meant. She couldn't understand what

16

was happening. The bugs had completely obscured the windows, the live ones crawling over the splattered remains, trying to get in. She felt the blood drain from her face. Could they? Would they find a way?

It felt obscene and somehow biblical in a very not-okay way. Reece still hadn't appeared, but a cry came from the kitchen, followed by a loud bang.

"That's a gun," Sal said, jumping.

*A gun?*

Roxanne shoved her fear aside and raced to the swinging door, calling out her brother's name as she ran. She burst into the kitchen, aware of Santo a few steps behind.

What she saw brought her to a skidding stop as she grappled with what she saw. Santo took her hand and tried to pull her back, but when she refused to budge, he gave up and angled his body in front of hers. Even a man his size couldn't block out the horror, though.

The oily tide coated the ceiling and lapped against the walls in the kitchen, stark against the stainless steel and new paint.

The back door stood wide open to the October night. The same back door that Reece and their older brother, Ryan, fought about constantly. Ryan insisted that it remained locked after five. Reece complained that Ryan was a control freak who needed to get a life. *"What the fuck does he care if the back door is open? For Christ sake, let the slaves have some fresh air."*

The shelving that held pots and pans had been knocked over, its contents scattered all around it. The dishwasher was sprawled beside the sink. She could only see his legs and feet, but she recognized the rolled-up jeans, bright yellow sneakers, and hem of his too-big Iron Man T-shirt bunched around his thighs. The black ooze splattered his inert form.

*Flash, flash, flash.* The images bombarded her so fast that she could barely focus on one before moving to another.

Reece stood in the doorway to the small office that was tucked between the walk-in refrigerator and the far wall, facing away from her. Through the big window that allowed an unobstructed view from the desk into the kitchen, she saw a man in front of the opened safe.

"You shot him. You fucking shot Manny," Reece shouted.

The man glanced over his shoulder at Reece, and Roxanne felt all the air leave her lungs. He wore a ski mask pulled down to hide his features, with black paint rimming his eyes. Only the whites and the pale blue irises could be seen. He'd sewn the mouth-hole closed with fat, ugly stitches so that not even his lips showed. He glanced past Reece to where Roxanne and the others now stood. Reece turned, too, and in the dread she saw on his face, Roxanne read so much more.

Reece knew this masked man. More than that, her brother had let him in.

Disbelief pierced her as the man spoke. His words came disembodied from behind the stitched mask and all the more terrifying for those frigid eyes in their obsidian setting.

"Trust me, Reece."

He shot her twin brother before she could grasp what he meant to do. Roxanne screamed again, but fear had closed her throat and all that emerged was a strangled cry. The echo of the gunfire reverberated through the kitchen, and her brother fell to the hard, tiled floor, his blood spilling from a fist-sized wound in his chest. Then the man with the ghastly mask spun and she looked into the pale eyes and knew that what lurked behind that frozen blue was not human.

Not human by any measure.

As if invited by the blood spilling from her brother's wound and the black gunk pooling on the floor, others began to pour in through the back door like roaches from a drain. Others. Not people but . . . She stared numbly, trying and failing to label what she saw. Whatever *they* were, they didn't wear masks. They didn't need to. Their appearance was hunched and gnarled, their skin so colorless it looked like paste. And their eyes . . . white except for the pinpoint of the pupil. White lanterns in the most gruesome faces she'd ever seen.

Santo jerked her away just as the man with the mask pulled the trigger two times in rapid succession and Sal and Jim hit the floor.

"No!" she cried as blood splattered her skin in a hot spray. Santo was dragging her through the swinging doors when something slammed into her from behind and she stumbled. Excruciating pain exploded through her, and Santo was all that kept her from falling.

He shouted something, but she couldn't make out the

words through the screeching agony. The pain became an entity that owned her.

She looked down to see that blood covered her pink Love's T-shirt and bubbled when she tried to suck in a breath. She'd been shot. Just like Reece . . . Her thoughts blurred and her knees gave.

Santo swept her into his arms as he raced across the dining room, charging into the bug-infested night. Roxanne felt herself slipping, *hurtling* toward a black unknown that felt ominously familiar. They'd met before, Roxanne and death, and she knew that in the darkness, she'd find someone waiting. He always waited, that nameless, faceless presence that welcomed and terrified her at once.

Santo called her name, and for a moment she was back with him, looking into his eyes, trying to read what she saw there. What did he have to do with all of this? In a sliver of lucidity, her mind connected a dot she didn't understand. Before she could decipher the hidden meaning, it was gone again.

She thought of her older brother and sister and began to cry. Her eyes squeezed tight against the pain that throbbed from inside out.

She released one last wheezing breath.

And then, for the fourth time in her life, Roxanne Love died.

# ABOUT THE AUTHOR

New York Times Bestselling author, Erin Quinn, writes dark paranormal romance for the thinking reader. Her books have been called "riveting," "brilliantly plotted" and "beautifully written" and have won, placed or showed in numerous awards. Look for the third book in the Beyond Series, The Seven Sins of Ruby Love in late 2015. Book One and Two, The Five Deaths of Roxanne Love and Three Fates of Ryan Love are available now.

Go to www.erinquinnbooks.com or more information or
https://www.facebook.com/ErinQuinnAuthor
Twitter @ErinQuinnAuthor.
Sign up for Erin Quinn's newsletter at
http://erinquinnbooks.com/Enter_maillist.htm
or enter Erin's monthly contest at
http://erinquinnbooks.com/Contest.htm
to be automatically added and eligible for free books.

# Books by Erin Quinn

**THE BEYOND SERIES:**

**THE FIVE DEATHS OF ROXANNE LOVE (BOOK 1)**
A Reaper finds that the women he came to kills is the one person he is willing to die to protect.

**THE THREE FATES OF RYAN LOVE (BOOK 2)**
Ryan Love is about to discover a fate too tempting to resist.

**THE SEVEN SINS OF RUBY LOVE, BOOK 3**
Coming soon.

**THE FORBIDDEN LIFE OF ALEX MOORE (NOVELLA 1.5)**
Alex must risk all to defend the woman he loves and the forbidden life he refuses to give up.

**THE RESURRECTION OF SAM SLOAN, NOVELLA 2.5**
Her heart tells her to trust him, but can Maggie ignore the voice inside, warning her of danger?

## THE MISTS OF IRELAND SERIES:

### HAUNTING BEAUTY (BOOK 1)
Caught between realms, neither dead or alive. Her life is about to change. His is about to begin.

### HAUNTING WARRIOR (BOOK 2)
He's trapped in a web of time, bound to the woman of his dreams. She captures his heart, but he must fight to save their future.

### HAUNTING DESIRE (BOOK 3)
In a world gone wrong, the only way to save everything he values, is to sacrifice the one woman he was meant to love.

### HAUNTING EMBRACE (BOOK 4)
Nothing can stop him from finding the woman who betrayed and imprisoned him for millennia. Nothing but his heart.

For a complete book list of Erin Quinn's titles, go to
http://www.erinquinnbooks.com

www.ingramcontent.com/pod-product-compliance
Lightning Source LLC
Chambersburg PA
CBHW060432130626
46555CB00005B/2317